The GEM LAKES

A Novel

The GEM LAKES

A Novel

Rob Keough

GREAT PLAINS
PUBLICATIONS

Copyright © 2005 Rob Keough

Great Plains Publications
420—70 Arthur Street
Winnipeg, MB R3B 1G7
www.greatplains.mb.ca

All rights reserved. No part of this publication may be reproduced or transmitted in any form or in any means, or stored in a database and retrieval system, without the prior written permission of Great Plains Publications, or, in the case of photocopying or other reprographic copying, a license from Access Copyright (Canadian Copyright Licensing Agency), 1 Yonge Street, Suite 1900, Toronto, Ontario, Canada, M5E 1E5.

Great Plains Publications gratefully acknowledges the financial support provided for its publishing program by the Government of Canada through the Book Publishing Industry Development Program (BPIDP); the Canada Council for the Arts; as well as the Manitoba Department of Culture, Heritage and Tourism; and the Manitoba Arts Council.

Design & Typography by Relish Design Studio Ltd.

Printed in Canada by Friesens

CANADIAN CATALOGUING IN PUBLICATION DATA

Main entry under title:

Keough, Rob
  The gem lakes / Rob Keough.

ISBN 1-894283-58-9

1. Title.

PS8621.E68G44 2005 jC813'.6 C2005-903321-5

To AM, who loaned a fourteen-year-old boy with a short-lived paper route enough money to buy his first computer and with it, his first word processor. Thirteen years later, I appreciate it even more.

To Ang, whose never ending queries of "Shouldn't you be writing?" were laced more with encouragement than harassment.

Many thanks and appreciation to KB and JG and to Murray, for happily answering a billion questions about writing in general. (Who can forget 'Grammar Night in Canada?')

This story was written in the spirit of BOBSHIRDON, the pale yellow cabin that sits beside a Lampshine Lake of its own. It may just be one of the best places on earth.

The Gem Lakes

- Lake of the Clouds
- Diamond Lake
- Ruby Lake
- Moonstone Lake
- "The Heights"
- Sapphire Lake
- Black Spruce Bog
- Emerald Lake
- Poplar / Birch
- Opal Lake
- Bay of Fangs
- Timber Wolf Lake
- Lampshine Lake

N

PART ONE

The old crow, sleek and black as oil, was perched on the top branch of a towering balsam tree. He had been watching the humans for a while now. They first appeared as a speck on the faraway dirt road, occasionally dipping out of sight on the deep bends and twisting turns, until finally, half an hour later, they pulled into the clearing that serves as Lampshine Lake's parking lot.

From its vantage point high above, the crow could see the humans unpacking their red mini-van and piling their bags into a small wheelbarrow, which the father was now struggling to control. He knew they would make several trips between the parking lot and the dock, as they did every year at this time, and load their gear into a boat that took them across the lake to the family cabin.

These are old friends—the Lucknows. This particular crow has set its beady eyes on them year after year, season after season. For some reason, this time is not the same. No, it is quite different. Something is not right at all. Not so much in Mrs. Lucknow's new hair style, or fifteen-year-old Claire's new CD, or the fact that Bob Lucknow has veered the wheelbarrow into the bush and tipped it over—the elderly bird has seen that one before—but most definitely in something else.

The GEM LAKES

The change lies in young Jake. One year younger than his sister, Jake is the near perfect model of a teenage boy. He is an encyclopedia of sports stats, can name every World Series winning team's starting line-up of the past ten seasons, and can throw a football hard enough to leave a red welt on his father's chest during a game of beach football.

His easy smile and his developing frame have caught the attention of more than a few of the young girls in his class, including Melissa Murray, who, if he were given the option, he would rather kiss than any of the others. If he could only work up the nerve to *talk* to her first, well, that might get the ball rolling. Jake did not know of a single girl that kissed a boy she hadn't talked to first.

Jake, at this moment, is thinking about none of these things. He is thinking about the one thing that has turned his typical teenage life completely upside down. It is the *thing* inside him that is taking his attention. The golfball sized *thing* that has attached itself and then grown onto his brain. The doctors called it a tumour. They called it an inoperable tumour.

Those words coming from the doctor's mouth had hit his parents like each letter was a poisonous dart, turning their stomachs and burning their eyes. It was Jake who had calmed them that day in the hospital and it was Jake who reassured them again whenever the strain threatened to break them down.

It had not been caused by anything Jake had breathed in or eaten, nor was it connected with anything Jake did or didn't do. It was simply a group of cells that grew out of control. These things happen on occasion. It was, in an ironic turn of phrase, the luck of the draw

Words like computerized axial tomography, malignant and radiation have invaded his vocabulary, taking the place of Barry Bonds' home run records, Minnesota Viking game statistics and second-tier swear words like "damn" or "blast". Instead of chocolate bars and chewing gum, he now carries a small red bottle of pills everywhere he goes. He must take three other pills to counteract the effects of the first one. The pills will manage his pain, but do little to prolong his life. Not to mention they make him feel, to put it lightly, as sick as a dog. Although, if you asked Jake, no dog had ever felt as sick as he had the last few weeks.

The crow tittered nervously on the thin balsam branch. Even though it was not quite sure what had drawn it to the boy in the first place, it is sure it has little to do with the dreadful cancer on his brain.

The Lucknows have not come here to avoid the unavoidable. It is a place that has meant peacefulness their entire lives, and they only hope it holds enough of it to get them through the summer.

"Sweet Mother of Mary!" cried Bob Lucknow. This would be the extent of his cursing in front of the children, but to the supreme irritation of his wife, it ranked among his favourite sayings. He usually only let it fly when he was tense. Finding himself face down in the bush for the second time today, Bob Lucknow was now officially tense.

"You'd think you would have learned your lesson the first time you piled the wheelbarrow too high," noted Susan, "and don't cuss in front of the children."

Bob mumbled something under his breath (something Jake could have sworn were another couple of cuss words, although a little more salty this time around), and brushed the dirt from his pants. Jake and Claire, also for the second time today, re-piled the bags on the wheelbarrow, careful not to stack them too high.

"Is this the last of it?" asked Jake. He was getting tired and just wanted to get across the lake and check out the cabin. It would be a welcome sight after the three-hour car trip. It would be well worth it.

"If your Mother didn't pack the kitchen sink, which I haven't come across yet, then yes, that is it."

The **GEM LAKES**

Susan threw her husband a menacing glance. "You're the one who had the backseat stuffed with fishing gear! It's a wonder you didn't try to strap the kids to the roof!"

"Susan, Susan, Susan. Jake and I are going for the big ones this year. What do you want us to do, tie some string to a stick?" Bob countered, lightly punching his son's arm as an act of solidarity.

It took another twenty minutes to load the boat. While the original red paint had long ago faded to pink, and the aluminum benches had not become any more comfortable to sit on, the old twenty horsepower motor started on the second try. "Old Reliable," Bob declared. The cabin was suddenly only five minutes away.

As they moved out onto the lake and reached planing speed, Claire stretched like a cat on the middle bench while Bob and Susan sat near the motor. The weight at the back of the boat lifted the tip, where Jake was sitting, imagining he was not in a boat at all, but flying above the surface of the water. Flying towards the cabin and away from the doctors.

The pale yellow cabin showed little signs of aging. It had stood on the very same spot for over eighty years, yet aside from some ancient, curled up shingles on the roof, it looked as sturdy as the day Jake's great-grandfather had built it. The fridge, which Bob was lighting now, the oven and the lamps were all propane-fuelled. Jake had to help his dad carry hundred-pound propane tanks all the way from the landing dock. They were heavy and awkward and not at the top of the list of Jake's favourite things to do.

Hydro crews had tried to put power lines through a long time ago, before Jake's grandfather was even born, but they had run into problems, about which, for some reason, his father would never go into detail. Their conversations about the subject usually went something like the one they were having now.

"Hey Dad, are they ever going to put power lines through here?"
"They tried once. They couldn't do it."
"Why not?"
"Too many trees in the way."

Jake was never easily put off, "But my friend Dave has a cabin at Raven Nest and they have power. There's just as many trees there!"

"It's different."

"How?"

"It just is, son."

"Why?"

At that point, Bob Lucknow's forehead would usually crunch into a wave of wrinkles, as it was at this very moment. "Does Dave have a T.V.? Does he have hot water? Does he have a telephone?"

"Yeah. Uh huh, Sure."

"Uh huh. Does he have propane lamps? Does he have to boil the water before doing the dishes? Does he even have an outhouse?"

"No."

"Exactly. I wouldn't trade any of those things for electricity. And if you took a vote, I don't think you'd find anybody on this lake that would either." Of course, he never answered why they had never finished putting the lines through to begin with, but he always managed to make Jake feel like he shouldn't have asked the question in the first place.

Jake did know that there were only twenty cabins on Lampshine. All of them had been passed on through several generations of families, almost all descendants of the original railroaders who had worked laying the main line. Jake knew the story well.

Back in 1912, a group of four surveyors for the Canadian railway broke through the bush and stood on the shore of what they would later name Lampshine Lake. Indeed, the main line would end up bordering the south side of the lake in the years to come, a line of steel set through a land speckled with small lakes, rolling granite and sturdy forests.

The majestic spell of Lampshine left none of the men unaffected. All four had built cabins on the lake within five years of that initial encounter...but they had not been the first.

The GEM LAKES

That first day the surveyors arrived, a crisp late May morning, the ice had completely retreated from the shore. One of the surveyors noticed a thin wisp of smoke curling above the north shore's jagged treeline.

As it turned out, the source of that smoke was the same dilapidated cabin that is still set into the forest, several hundred metres away from what would be the future Lucknow property. There was a trapper even then—Elias "Chipper" Prefontaine. It was never known how long he had been there, only that he had disappeared in the winter of '35.

The campers and cottage owners all assumed he had died somewhere in the boundless forest behind them, which had been declared a wilderness zone by the Canadian government in 1929. There was much discussion about ripping the cabin down. In the end, it was decided that it was an important historical part of the lake, so they let it rot instead.

It would no doubt have crumbled into the ground if the next trapper had not come along three years after that and claimed the structure. He repaired the place so that it was liveable throughout the year and trapped out of it to this very day, sixty-five years after taking over.

Back then, nobody had bothered to ask his name. He never offered it and people usually treated him much like they did the bears—they knew they were in the woods, but never wanted to come across them while they were out on a walk. So the cottagers took it upon themselves to call him "The Mad Trapper," a fairly unoriginal title, conjured up, coincidentally, by the eldest son of the man who had come up with "Chipper" some years earlier.

Until five years ago, when the twenty families banded together and paid to have a ten-kilometre road set through the bush, the only way in or out of Lampshine was by train or float plane.

The train worked well until the railway cut the weekend service, causing hours of delays and staggered pick-ups that left some people late for work on the Monday. Jake could remember his parents sending the entire summer's worth of supplies down in the spring and then shipping whatever was left back to the city in the fall.

The road had major advantages to the rail, not the least of which was that you could enter and leave the lake according to your own schedule, even in the middle of the week. But Jake held a soft spot for the train rides up, and especially for those summer days when one of the neighbours would be building an addition on their cabin or a new shed. The whole lake would gather at the train station and help unload a boxcar full of lumber, making a human chain from the track to the dock. It was a social event in itself. Jake's generation would never see anything like it again.

Jake was having a "bad" day. It started that morning, when he blacked out and fell brushing his teeth. His parents, who had seen more than their fair share of this over the past year, picked him up and put him back in bed until noon. He thought he had caught a glimpse of Claire crying on the way down the hall, but he was still a little foggy. "It's the tumour pressing against certain parts of his brain. You might expect hallucinations and more frequent blackouts. I recommend keeping him in the hospital." The doctor's advice was sound but cold. Jake had grown up at Lampshine Lake. He had spent most of his summers there. His sickness was incurable, his parents were devastated, but were they going to hook him up to a machine for his last few weeks, or were they going to let him live his life the way he wanted to? His doctor had agreed, as long as he carried that little red bottle of pain pills.

It was that exact same little red bottle of pills that Jake was now tying up with a fishing line. He was sitting in the front of the family's birch bark canoe, the one his dad had made especially for Jake and Claire. It was smaller than a normal canoe and also much lighter, making it possible for the two kids to portage short distances by themselves. Jake usually liked to guide the canoe from the back, but on this day, he was too drained to even hold the paddle.

The GEM LAKES

Jake laid his paddle across his lap, and was concentrating on twisting the fishing line around the bottle for the ninth or tenth time. Satisfied it would hold, he secured it with three small knots. As a finishing touch, he removed five medium-sized weights from his Stream Master tackle box and clipped them onto the line right above the bottle.

"Are you going to fish or what?"

Claire was prodding her brother from the back with the butt end of her paddle. She had the same sandy-brown hair as her younger brother, with chocolate brown eyes to match. They were mistaken for twins all the time.

She had seen him black out before but that wasn't what bothered her now. It was the frequency of the blackouts. Since they had arrived at the lake last week, he had collapsed three times. She didn't want to think about what that meant.

"Yeah, yeah, I'm deciding on a colour," Jake responded without turning around.

Claire was not easily put off, and as they slowly let the current take them for a while, she tried to start up another conversation.

"There's the old trapper. Do you think he's spying on us?"

Jake looked up just as he snapped his last weight on the line and glanced over to the shore. There it was—the Mad Trapper's cabin. It was the last one on the lake before the endless forest began. And there *he* was, sitting on a rotten chair on his decrepit old cabin's sagging porch. It was probably only the third time he had ever seen the old man. He looked a hundred years old. Any hair he had left was tucked underneath an old greasy baseball cap, the kind that had webbed mesh on the back, and just sat on top of your head. He did not wave, he merely watched. Jake and Claire did not wave either. They had been told to stay away from the old man.

The Mad Trapper (they didn't know his name) had set trap lines along the back rivers and even down through the Gem Lakes. He had once been Jake's grandfather's best friend, really his only friend, before his death twenty-five years ago.

The *thing* had been inside of Grandpa too. Cancer, however, had not killed him. The Mad Trapper had. At least that was the rumour. The trapper and Grandpa Lucknow went on a canoe trip through the Gem Lakes, and two weeks later, only the Mad Trapper came back. The police had been involved, and the trapper had been sent away somewhere (the insane asylum, his dad had told Jake once), but he had been released only five years later.

Jake turned his attention back to the task at hand. They were passing the rocks. Jake pressed the release trigger on his rod and flicked it to his right, towards the shore. The red bottle flashed once in the light of the sun and then skipped across the water four times before it followed the weights below the surface. Jake waited until almost all his line was out and then tightened the drag until the tension could go no more. Any second now.

With two more long strokes of the paddle, Claire had covered about eight metres of water, and Jake felt the bottle bounce on the rocks at the bottom of the lake.

Please, please, please....

With a couple of more paddle strokes, the bottle finally wedged between two rocks. As soon as Jake felt it get stuck he pulled on the rod, wedging it even further. With the tension of the rod set too tight, the line snapped in the blink of an eye.

"Oh no! A snag!" Jake cried, trying to sound disappointed.

Claire was not impressed. "You know the rock shelf is over there. Why would you cast into it? What's wrong with you?"

"High risk, high reward."

"What does that mean?"

"It means that the biggest fish are in the riskiest spots. Like in weeds or around rocks. You can't get the big ones without the occasional snag."

Claire thought this over for a moment and seemed to follow the logic.

Jake turned around to find more line in his tackle box, feeling better than he had in months. As young as he was, he had been able to accept his illness to some degree. He had not, however, been willing to be nauseous and weak for what precious time he had left. The pills were supposed to control pain but in return stole Jake's appetite and made him feel like he had a very bad flu twenty-four hours a day. As he glanced back to the shore, he noticed that the Mad Trapper had disappeared from his chair, which was now rocking by itself in the slight breeze. Jake shivered. He could hear the chair creaking, even from out on the lake.

Bob and Susan had first met at Lampshine Lake. Susan's family often came for summer visits on the train to stay in their cousin's cabin on Lot Eight while they were off "touring" the European countryside. They had not been the first, and they would not be the last of the romances that had sparked and blossomed during summers at Lampshine Lake.

Bob Lucknow now made his living selling office supplies. Many of his customers had been with him for years. As far as things like toilet paper and paper towels went, it was all about the salesman. People wouldn't change suppliers over a few pennies as long as they were getting good service. He had received forty-six cards of sympathy from his various clients before he left on a leave of absence for three months.

Susan Lucknow had been going to night school to become a real-estate agent when Claire came along. She put work aside and quickly found that the challenge of being a mother was more than enough to take up the hours of her day. She quit night school. She and Bob decided to have another child a year later, and although that effort stretched into the following year, Jake was finally born, completely healthy, a few days after Christmas. He led a very happy life until that terrible day that he first started complaining about double-vision and blinding headaches.

It was the fresh morning air that was the biggest distinction between the city and the lake. When Jake first woke up in the morning and felt the cool air through the open window, he was completely refreshed. Even more than that, he felt recharged. It wasn't like waking up in the city in a stuffy house, feeling like a slug.

If the crisp air didn't get him out of bed, then the lure of breakfast cooking on the old woodstove did. With the smell of fresh fish frying in the skillet, bacon snapping and cracking right beside them, and a pan full of eggs beside those, it wasn't hard to be a morning person at the lake.

"Good morning, honey, did you have a good sleep?" his mom asked. Jake had slept for eleven hours. He nodded his head.

"Did you take your pill yet this morning?"

"Yeah Mom, it's kinda hard to forget," he responded, trying to sound bored. If they were handing out Oscars, he might have snagged one for that little performance. His mother smiled and turned her attention to the eggs and frowned. Her sunny-side ups were in the advanced stages of over-easiness…again.

"Where's Dad?"

"Where do you think? He's fishing with the Morley brothers again. What's on your schedule for today Jake?"

He held his plate out as she scooped two pickerel fillets and some bacon strips and slid them on. He declined the eggs.

"Nothing much. Might do some exploring maybe."

"You should go past the creek. Find me some new blueberry bushes. The ones around here are bare. I can make pie tonight if you get enough."

Jake loved blueberry pie. He quickly agreed to hunt down some berries in return for two large pieces of pie for himself.

Just then, his father rambled in the front door, wearing his fishing hat and an old tattered vest that used to be Jake's grandfather's.

"Hey sport! Where's your sister?"

"In bed, as usual." This was a fact. Claire did not believe in getting up before the crack of noon if she could help it. "How was fishin'?"

"Great. It's always great with those Morleys. They sure know the spots."

Jake nodded but noticed that his dad was noticeably empty-handed, "Well, where's the fish then?"

"I let the boys keep 'em. They're feeding three."

Jake nodded again.

"It smells fantastic in here. What's for breakfast?"

"Fish, bacon and eggs…over-easy, just the way you like them."

His father stole a glance at Jake and rolled his eyes. His favourite was sunny-side up.

"Jake's going exploring today Bob. He's going to rustle up some blueberries for dessert tonight."

Bob Lucknow hung his fishing hat on a peg that resembled a woodpecker and gave his wife a look that was half concern and half curiosity.

"Exploring huh? Where are you headed Jake?"

Jake finished chewing the last of his bacon. "I don't know. Past the creek maybe."

Caribou Creek flowed into Lampshine Lake from Timber Wolf Lake, which was fed by another, smaller creek connected to the Gem Lakes. The Lucknows had camped on several of the islands on Timber Wolf, but had never gone farther than that. Jake sometimes wondered if his dad had ever been back there, but he would never ask. Not after what happened to Grandpa.

"You just be careful in that creek buddy. Those rocks are slippery."

"I know, I know."

"Stick to the trails. It's easy to get turned around in the bush."

"Yes, Dad, can I go now?"

"Sure, have fun."

"I will."

Jake turned around just before he made it to the back door. "Hey Dad, maybe we can go fishing when I get back?"

"Sure thing bud. Try to make it back by four then. It's prime time fishing at that hour."

Susan rolled her eyes.

Fun was not the main purpose of Jake's exploration. It was sometimes just nice to get away from people, especially if you needed to think. The creek ran just behind the Lucknow's cabin, so it was not long before Jake was testing his balance, crossing the narrow water on a fallen tree. He walked with one foot ahead of the other and when he felt his weight shift either way, he held his arms out like wings to keep his footing.

He felt a small adrenaline rush when he made the last step off the log and set off towards the trails, banging an empty ice cream pail against his leg like a tambourine. The trail was well worn and it was not long before he could feel the cool breeze from Timber Wolf through the trees. A few minutes later, he could actually see the big lake in the not-so-far distance. He kept going, intent on walking farther down the path than usual this time. If there was anything new to see, now was the time to see it.

He strolled past the old tree fort, which his dad had officially condemned two summers ago, and past Kissing Creek, which he and Claire had nicknamed after busting their twenty-year- old cousin Amanda making out with Gus Clump from Lot Six that same year. He stopped to watch a garter snake slither in front of him and disappear into the underbrush, pausing only for a moment to stick its forked tongue out at him. He carried on through a patch of wild grass that in turn caused him to stop and pick off dozens of burrs that had attached themselves to his pants.

He zigged and zagged through the thinning trail, stepping off occasionally to inspect any blueberry bushes that he saw. Most of them were sparse to say the least. He was not going home empty-handed, that was for sure. He had already primed his stomach for fresh blueberry pie and there could be no acceptable substitute for that.

It is not hard, especially if you are a daydreamer, to get lost in your thoughts. It is even easier, if you *are* a daydreamer, and you *have* gotten lost in your thoughts, to get lost in the woods, or wherever you happen to be at the time.

Jake had just realized that he had wandered farther off the main path than he had planned, and had gotten himself completely turned around. He tried to split the blame for his current conundrum between the fact that he had seen absolutely no blueberry bushes worth stopping at, and the fact that for the last hour and a half he had been throwing a perfect game in game seven of the World Series…at least in his head.

Back to the present time, however. Jake started whistling nervously, trying to convince himself that he wasn't lost at all.
He walked a few more minutes up the trail, looking for something that he recognized. Maybe the old tree swing that dad had broken three years ago when he had tried it for the first time since he was sixteen. The extra hundred pounds had snapped the tree limb like a toothpick. His mother had only stopped laughing about it a week ago.

He saw nothing he remembered, but he did step off the path just long enough to discover an overflowing berry bush. He bent down and started plucking purple blueberries, hopeful that when his parents came looking for him, at least he would have something to deflect their anger.

He was not entirely worried, but being alone in the bush was a little uncomfortable, especially since he kept hearing the unnerving sound of the wind through the trees all around him. Just the wind, he thought to himself, just the wind.

Just as Jake had nearly half a pail of berries (and had eaten about the same), he heard a terrible noise. A crashing that was coming straight for him. He dropped the ice cream pail, half the berries spilling on the mossy rocks under his feet. *This is it*, he thought, *a huge wild animal is going to maul me. This is how it's going to end.* He froze and as he did, a rush of calm rippled over his thoughts. Of all the terrible things that have happened to him, what was one more? Pour it on, baby!

Who was he kidding? He was terrified! He turned around and ran. Unfortunately, his foot caught the root of an old oak tree, and he fell to the ground in a heap. A graceful escape it was not.

There was a horrendous groaning sound followed by a resounding crash. A tree landed ten feet from his head; branches and bark and leaves exploded off the tree and covered his back. The trunk was at least a foot thick and twenty feet long. Jake did not move, bracing himself for another tree to fall around him. It did not come.

He scrambled to his feet and was about to give his original escape plan another go when he noticed the Mad Trapper standing in the woods watching him. He was holding a feeble looking band saw—a harp, only a blade where the string should be, his arms covered in sawdust. It was the closest that Jake had ever seen him.

They just looked at each other in strange silence for about a minute, like they were sizing each other up. Jake would have been terrified if this had been a year ago, but something inside him had changed and the old trapper didn't seem as threatening. Besides, he was smaller than Jake had imagined. He looked older too. He had more creases in his face than an unmade bed.

The old man spoke in a raspy, gravelly voice like passed-over sandpaper. "What brings you this deep in the woods, boy?"

Jake hesitated for only a moment, "I...I was looking for blueberries," he nodded towards the bush, half of which was now crushed by the tree. "How about yourself?" he offered bravely.

The old man said nothing. None of the cottagers had talked to him in years. He reached behind his back and pulled out a hatchet. The sharp edge gleamed in a ray of sunshine.

For the second time in five minutes, Jake's temporary courage evaporated.

The trapper seemed to ignore him, however, and went about chopping the branches off the thick tree trunk. He made quick, short swings, causing wood chips and branches to whiz past his head. The last time Jake and his father had cut down a tree for firewood, it had taken them all afternoon to clean it. The old man was almost done.

Jake was fascinated, and hadn't even realized that he had edged to within six feet of the trapper, who was now hammering large spikes into the trunk with the flat end of the hatchet. The trapper then removed a worn leather harness from his pack and attached it to the spikes. He looked up at Jake. "You've got it in you too, don't you?"

At first, Jake didn't know what he was talking about. Then he realized with amazement the man was referring to his tumour. How did he know?

"I've got somethin' back at the cabin that you might be interested in. If you're not scared, that is."

"I'm not scared." Jake's mouth responded too quickly for his brain.

The trapper nodded, and slipped the harness over his shoulders. He was dragging the tree back to his cabin. "This way then. It's not such a far way."

Jake watched in fascination as the trapper pulled the tree behind him like an ox. He must be a lot stronger than he looked. Jake tried his best to help out, pushing the tree from the other end, completely forgetting about his mother's ice cream pail. He wasn't sure he was contributing much, but he hoped the Mad Trapper appreciated the effort.

From the outside, the trapper's log cabin looked like it had been abandoned for years. Two broken windowpanes were covered with yellowed newspapers, the roof was a green and brown patchwork of moss, and Jake thought he could even see through some of the cracks in the wall. Jake was pretty sure that the place must be haunted.

The trapper himself seemed no worse for wear after hauling the massive log through the woods. After brushing the harness off his shoulders, he wiped his brow with the sleeve of his jacket and started walking towards the cabin, presumably leaving the log cutting for later. He just waved at Jake to follow.

Jake hesitated again at the door, before stepping through and entering into what might have been a completely different universe. The cabin smelled like a bakery. There was homemade bread on the woodstove. The smell of fresh ground coffee filled Jake's nostrils. He liked the smell and it made him realize how weak his parents' designer cappuccino was.

He also noticed four pails overflowing with all kinds of berries—blueberries, raspberries, cranberries, all literally the size of ping-pong balls. Where had he found those?

There was a gigantic moose head set high on one wall, whose eyes seemed to follow Jake wherever he stepped. Jake would not like to have met *that* in the woods in its day.

There were unusually large turtle shells, weasel skulls, deer antlers, and a very strange white beaver that had been stuffed and was now cluttered on top of a shelf in the corner.

"Albino," the old man said.

"Excuse me?"

"The beaver. It's albino. White pigment."

"Oh. I didn't know they came that way."

"You'd be surprised."

The old man shuffled behind the counter, reached into a metal bucket and pulled something out. Jake couldn't tell what it was at first.

The Mad Trapper of Lampshine Lake held up two cans for inspection. Root beer.

Jake must have looked hesitant because the old man rasped, "Don't worry. It's fully loaded—sugar, caffeine, rat poison. All the things you expect from a crazy trapper."

"Mad," Jake corrected.

"What's that now?"

"Mad Trapper, not crazy."

"Right…mad." He motioned to Jake to sit and he brought the cans over. Jake looked around him and checked out his seating options.

There was a rickety old rocking chair that Jake figured would be good for one "rock" before he flipped completely over, an ancient couch, which was covered by a large wolf skin and a small stool that was basically a hand-sanded tree stump.

He chose the wolf couch and was surprised at how thick the fur was. He tilted away from the head so he didn't have to look at its menacing face.

The old man pulled up the rocking chair. Jake couldn't tell if it was the chair or the trapper that was creaking and cracking as he sat. Up close for the first time, Jake studied the Mad Trapper more carefully. His jawline and chin were landscaped with hard white stubble that looked as rough as a brillo pad. His nose sloped sharply from his dark sunken eyes and his hands were rough and scarred, twisted highways of veins and muscles. Jake figured that those hands could bend steel without much effort.

The trapper never smiled but when he spoke Jake could see that his teeth were as yellow as corn kernels. He tried not to stare. After all, it was probably tough to find good dental care out here.

Jake waited until the old man took a sip of his root beer before he tried his own. It was cold, very cold and very good! He was surprised at how thirsty he was. He had been out in the woods since he had left home and that had been a few hours ago. He took three long sips.

"Your Grandpa had it in him. Just like you. People said I killed him. You believe that?"

Jake stopped in mid-sip. The Mad Trapper didn't beat around the bush. Right then and there, Jake decided that he did not believe it. "No, I don't believe it."

The trapper considered that.

"They put me in Irondale for a spell. Do you know what that is?"

Jake did not.

"It's where they put the loons. I wasn't crazy when I went in there, but I'll tell you something—they tried their hardest to make me that way. First time I seen electricity in my life and they ran it through *me* more than the lamps…the things I saw in that place…"

"But why'd they put you in there if you didn't kill my Grandpa?"

The trapper eyed him carefully, "Because of what I've seen back there…what I told 'em I seen." He nodded towards the back door, as if the Gem Lakes began as soon as you stepped out of his cabin.

"People don't believe what they haven't seen for themselves, what they don't *choose* to believe in. It keeps 'em from being scared. Either way I didn't care if they believed me or not…as long as they didn't poke their noses 'round here…for too long at least."

Jake believed the trapper, but the obvious question remained, "Well, what happened to him then? Were you with him?"

The Mad Trapper of Lampshine Lake sat back in the rocking chair. There was a long silence.

"Your grandfather and I shared a trap line on the north shore of Timber Wolf. Beaver, muskrat, mink, that kind of thing."

Jake hung on to every word. His father had not told him much about his Grandpa. He nodded in fascination.

"We also started setting quite a few snares for wolf. Prime furs in the cold season. You could fetch a good price for a decent-sized timber. You know how to catch a wolf?"

Jake shook his head. Why would he even *think* about catching a wolf?

"Let me tell you boy, it's no easy task. They're smarter than most people. First you got to find a path that a pack might fancy. That could take weeks of scoutin'. Then, you tie a snare between two trees, overhanging that path. You got to hope that a wolf not only walks down that very path, but sticks his noggin right through your loop. If it does, it's trapped. If it don't, which it usually don't…you try again."

The trapper nodded to himself. "Well, Gordon and I got quite good at it. Your Grandpa—he had a nose for things like that. We snared three wolves in one winter. That's good…real good…" The trapper's raspy voice was fading more to a whisper. He hadn't talked this much in a very long time. "The problem was there was never much left by the time we got there."

"What do you mean?"

"Three times we went out to check the line. Three times we found a wolf's decapitated head in our snares. We found what was left of the meat a little ways in the bush…just ribs and gristle…and a whole lot of blood."

"What eats a wolf?" Jake asked, not sure if he wanted to know the answer.

"Anything can *eat* a wolf. What can kill it? That's the question."

"But I thought they were trapped. Wouldn't it be easy to kill them?"

He chuckled. "You ain't ever seen an animal in a trap line, have you son?"

Jake shook his head.

"The snare just holds 'em…and makes 'em madder than heck. Nowadays we got more humane traps, and that's a good thing. But back then…Anyway, I ain't seen nothin' that can tear apart something like that. Not a badger, not a bear, nothin'."

There was another long pause. Jake could hear the sound of surf, actually the rustle of aspens in the breeze. The trapper slowly nodded his head. "Gordon and I started huntin' this thing that killed the wolves and it took us right deep into the Gem Lakes. By the time we got to the Lake of the Clouds, your Gramps didn't feel no pain any more. He didn't look so bad either. I figure that's why he wanted to stay. I came back by myself."

"You mean you left him alive?"

"Sure I did. But them police don't want to believe such things—that a man would want to live in the bush. They didn't find a body because there was none to find."

"But people went looking for him."

"Those lakes have a way boy, a way of cutting searches short. Besides, if a man don't want to be found in the bush, he won't be found."

"So you left him to die in the woods…alone?"

"Die? Who said anything 'bout dying? I played crib with him three weeks ago by Sapphire Lake."

Three weeks ago! "But Grandpa was sick. He had cancer like me." *That was over twenty-five years ago.*

"Yeah he did. I guess them doctors was wrong."

As Jake tried to digest this, the trapper got up and made his way to an old pine chest across the room. He lifted the stained brass latch and pulled out a yellowed piece of parchment. He held it for a moment and then brought it back to his chair. It was a map.

"The Gem Lakes," he announced. "The last piece of *real* wild frontier left on earth."

Jake studied the map carefully. At the bottom was Lampshine Lake, and though it wasn't marked, he quickly found the cove where his cabin was. He followed the small line that was Caribou Creek right into Timber Wolf. Right behind the northeast corner of that lake, was the first of seven other lakes that Jake had never seen on any other map. Not even on the aerial photograph that hung on the wall at the Lucknow cabin. The area behind Timber Wolf showed up as a huge swampy forest, a blur.

"Those first six are the Gem Lakes, as you can tell by their names."

Jake looked at the faded black ink that marked each body of water—Opal, Emerald, Sapphire, Diamond, Ruby and Moonstone. The seventh was called Lake of the Clouds and was by far the smallest of them all.

"Your grandfather is probably here right now." The trapper pointed a long, bony finger at the small lake. "He don't wander far from home no more."

Jake's mind was racing as fast as his heart. The map, as faded and tattered as it was, was the most inspiring thing that Jake had seen in his life.

There were notes jotted all around the marks and lines of the map, now mostly illegible, and symbols and drawings that had no meaning to Jake.

"We made that map ourselves, over many, many years. Your Grandpa and I."

"What are these symbols?" Jake pointed to a set of triangular marks near the second lake.

"The bear caves. Great rocks that have split and cracked over the years. The bears moved in 'bout fifty years ago and haven't left since."

Jake decided right there that he would not ask about the other symbols. He perhaps should have asked questions, all the questions he could possibly think of, but he was distracted by the Lake of the Clouds, where Gordon Lucknow was apparently alive and well.

"There are three things to remember about those lakes. One, take everything you've ever known and experienced on Lampshine Lake and put it behind you. Nothing here holds true over there."

"Second, grow eyes in the back of your head. Be mindful...at *all* times. Thirdly, and most important, don't go alone, under any circumstances. If nobody will go with you, don't go. There are things back there that are better not faced alone."

Jake, who had never even said he was going, now realized that he was. Of course he was. "Will you take me?" he asked.

The old trapper chuckled softly. "I'm afraid that my last trip back *was* my last trip back. I'm too old for those goin' ons."

He picked up the map. "Take this with you. Don't get lost."

Jake was hoping for a little better advice than "don't get lost". The map itself looked like it was about to fall apart. The trapper seemed to read his mind.

"Don't worry, she's in good shape. That parchment's held tight for more moons than you've ever seen."

Jake stood up, holding the map as if it were a priceless artifact. Maybe it was. He thanked the Mad Trapper for the root beer and the map and made his way towards the door.

"Take a pail of berries for your mother. She'll wonder why you've been so long."

Jake thanked him once more and headed towards the edge of the clearing, in the direction of his cabin. He carefully tucked the map away in his shirt pocket and was careful not to spill any of the jumbo berries. His mother would be out of her mind with excitement and more importantly, it might be worth a few more slices for him. Before he stepped into the woods he turned around and asked the trapper the question that had been gnawing on his mind.

"Did you ever find what killed those wolves?"

The trapper hung his head slightly, "It found us…don't ask too many questions boy. You'll scare yourself right out of those lakes before you even lay eyes on them."

Only a few minutes late, Jake shrugged the bright orange lifejacket over his shoulders and made his way to the dock, where his father was now standing, examining the water. His mother was back in the kitchen, gawking at the oversized berries, too surprised to admonish him for his tardiness.

They were about to embark on their first serious fishing expedition of the season. By serious, it meant that they weren't coming back until the stringer was full—or the sun went down—whichever occurred first.

"Come here, Jake, look at this." His father motioned a hand to where he was standing at the end of the dock.

There was a shadowy blob set against the dark bottom of the lake. In the blink of an eye, it bolted under the cover of the dock. A fish.

"It's a fish?"

Bob shook his head solemnly. "It's not just any fish...it's *the* fish. It's that smallmouth bass that's been eluding me for twenty years. Each year, it grows an inch or so bigger, and each year it aggravates me even more..."

Jake did not ask questions when his father started in on his fishing narratives. He knew all about this particular bass. His father had tried every lure in his tackle box, every colour of jig, one-tailed and two-tailed worms, cranks, spinners and minnows. He had once even saved a piece of prime rib roast and hooked it on his line. He had caught the snapping turtle instead. Now *that* had been an entertaining show.

"It lives under *my* dock, hangs out here all the time, probably has a nest right by *my* shoreline...I wouldn't be surprised if it's watching us right now...snickering and carrying on," he ranted, peering over his shoulder like the bass was planning a sneak attack. Bob motioned for Jake to untie the front of the boat as he did the same at the stern. Within moments, they were at the opposite shore, trolling the pickerel holes for next day's breakfast.

Bob Lucknow enjoyed nothing more than a good day of fishing. He could spend all day on the water, from sunrise to sundown with no breaks in between. Although, since his marriage eighteen years ago, that practice had come to a crashing halt.

Bob always wore his dad's old fishing vest and a hat that was absolutely covered in colourful flies. Bob did not fly fish, nor did he have a clue how to tie one either. He just liked the way they looked on his hat, so he went out and bought a new fly every year, just to add to the collection. This year's addition was a green and purple number that he attached right in the front.

Jake loved fishing as well, but in a vastly different way. Jake *hated* touching fish...not because they were slimy, or that they flopped around all over the place, but because of a traumatic incident back when he was just six years old. He had caught his first fish, a medium-sized pickerel, and his father had carefully netted it for him at the side of the boat.

He had been glowing with pride at his son, as Jake had gone to take the fish from him for a picture of his first catch. Unfortunately, in his excitement, Jake grabbed the fish by the still spiked fin that ran down the fish's back. He cut eight of his ten fingers on the sharp points, the slices deep like paper cuts only worse. They fell right over the joints of his fingers, so whenever he moved them, they reopened and stung wildly. It had taken him over a week to heal. He had never forgotten that pain and had developed a lingering fear that existed to this very day.

Catching fish, however, was not the point to Jake. It was the act of fishing that he loved, being out on the open water with his dad, watching the drama that unfolded every time his father got a nibble. *Oh c'mon, I got you baby! Nibble, nibble that's right, come to papa, just a little more, Ah! Gotcha! Jake get the net! SWEET MOTHER OF MARY GET THE NET!*

Jake actually went to great lengths to make sure he never pulled in another fish again. His tackle box was filled with Red Devils, those red spoons with the white stripe down the middle, twenty-one in all. He had snipped the tips of every hook, so that he would never be able to set it. As an extra precaution, he liked to tie them with a single loop knot, so that if a fish did happen to grab his lure, the line would easily break. He had lost more lures than he could remember. He stopped counting at thirty-eight. His dad would just shake his head every time. "Son, if you lose one more spoon, there's going to be more Red Devils at the bottom of this lake than hell itself."

Bob Lucknow did not consider himself a fool, nor was he blind, although with the mid-afternoon sun hanging high in a cloudless sky, he was thankful for his oversized sunglasses. If not for them, he would have to squint to watch his only son select yet another Red Devil out of his tackle box and tie it loosely to the doomed fishing line.

There was nothing Bob could say or do to convince Jake to handle fish again. Oh, how he had tried. The kid just couldn't get over the trauma of his first experience. He had absolutely no idea of the thrill he was missing.

Bob watched Jake cast his line out and eye the tip of his rod anxiously. The fact that he liked being out on the lake with his old man made Bob feel good. Maybe especially so, considering that he never caught any fish.

If Jake was less talkative than usual, it was only because his thoughts were completely consumed by his visit with the Mad Trapper. He would show Claire the map tonight and convince her to go with him. He would rather go with his friend Dave, but he had gone to his own cabin for the summer. There was nobody else his age at Lampshine and he would need *somebody*. His options were severely limited at this point.

Claire was the kind of sister who would tell you if you had something caught between your teeth...but only an hour after she first noticed it, allowing Jake to look like a fool for a full sixty minutes. But they were close otherwise. Being only one year apart had meant that they shared the same friends and played the same sports.

Between getting home from the trapper's cabin and stepping into the boat at the dock, Jake had come up with a million questions that he should have asked the Mad Trapper. He bit his lip and resisted asking his dad, even though he had said that he had never been back past Timber Wolf. Questions would surely arouse suspicion. Jake's train of thought was interrupted by his father's booming voice, "SWEET MOTHER OF MARY! GRAB THE NET JAKE! IT FEELS LIKE A MONSTER!"

Jake reeled in his own line and calmly picked up the net. He had seen this movie many times before. His dad managed to bring the fish to the side of the boat where Jake netted it easily. It was two, maybe three pounds, on the outside.

Bob looked disappointed. "It sure *felt* like a monster..."

Jake smiled, "That's okay Dad, seven more and we've got breakfast."

"I talked to him."

Claire, close to sleep, flipped over to find her brother's head hanging over the top bunk, a flashlight illuminating his face, making him look like a deranged, oversized bat.

"Who?" she inquired wearily.

"The Mad Trapper. I talked to him today."

Claire sat up straight, "What do you mean you talked to him? We're not supposed to go near him."

"He's actually pretty nice. He gave me a root beer."

Claire was aghast. "You drank it. I'm telling Mom. It was probably poison!"

"Sshhh," hushed Jake, "Do I look dead to you? I was in his cabin too."

"You went in his cabin! You are in so much trouble!"

"Sshhhh! I'm trying to tell you something!"

For the next half an hour, Jake told in exact detail (with maybe a few embellishments) how he had come across the trapper in the bush, how the tree had nearly hit him, and how the old man had dragged it back by himself. He told of the rickety cabin, how it was so different than they had pictured it on the inside, the animals, the giant berries, and the wolf skin couch. Then he told her what the trapper had said about Grandpa, and about the Gem Lakes.

"That's not funny Jake. Grandpa died a long time ago. He shouldn't be telling you ghost stories like that."

"It's not a ghost story. Look at this." Jake pulled out the fragile map and handed it to his sister. Together, they inspected it under the beam of the flashlight. "I've got a plan but I need your help. He told me not to go alone."

Claire knew where he was going with this so she decided to cut him off right then and there.

The GEM LAKES

"There is no way I'm going back there. No way Jose."

Jake had expected that reply. He would have to play dirty and throw out his trump card. "Well, I'm going with or without you. It's your call."

Claire thought this over for what seemed like an eternity. Jake knew what was coming next. He clicked the flashlight off so she wouldn't be able to see him rolling his eyes. "Let's see what the Ouiji board says."

The Ouiji board. To Jake, it was what it was, a plain board with a paper top. It had the alphabet printed on it with the words YES, NO and GOODBYE. There was a small, three-legged plastic "indicator" in the shape of a heart that had felt-tipped legs so the piece slid easily on the paper.

To Claire, the board was a way to communicate with trapped-on-earth spirits and long dead relatives. He had tried the board with her a few times with no results, apparently, Claire said, because he was disrespectful to the spirits. Their dad tried every spring to get the board to tell him if his beloved Detroit Tigers would win the World Series that fall. The board had never answered YES (it had never answered him at all actually) and the Tigers had never taken home the Series either. Bob Lucknow took the board's persistent silence as the spirit world's personal grudge against his favourite team.

Nonetheless, she had already pulled the board from beneath her bed. He would play along if that were what it took for her to go with him.

Claire whispered her usual directions. "Be respectful, and don't ask stupid questions. If you laugh, I'll break your arm." Jake, for some reason, did not feel like laughing tonight.

They were sitting across from each other on the cold hardwood floor, their fingers resting lightly on the indicator, eyes glued to the board of letters, which was dimly lit by two stubby candles. Their shadows flickered grotesquely and enormously on the wall. Jake had to admit that the board certainly gave him the creeps, especially in the half-dark.

"Is anybody there?" Claire inquired in a hushed voice. Very creepy. Jake was watching his sister's hands carefully, looking for the telltale movement of muscles that would come if she tried to push the marker herself and try to trick him.

"Is anybody there?"

Still nothing. Jake was thankful, he didn't want anything to happen. He was afraid that Claire, in exploring her dark side, would ask some morbid question whose answer would spook her from the trip. Her eyes were closed, concentrating with what seemed to be a ridiculous amount of effort for a board game. Jake, who had to mentally remind himself that he did not believe in the spirit world, nonetheless found his heart pounding against his ribs. He hoped that Claire could not hear it.

"Is anybody there?"

The marker shifted; only an inch at first, but then in two slow looping circles over the surface of the board. Jake was wide-eyed. Claire still had hers closed. His first reaction was to pull his hands off the indicator, but his cursed curiosity wouldn't let him.

"Who am I talking to?" she inquired.

The marker made another slow loop and then slowly spelled out a phrase. Jake lost the wording after the third letter. Claire did not. She whispered, "It said, who do you want me to be?"

"Holy smokes!" Jake blurted automatically. He was embarrassed but Claire just flashed him a 'Shut up, I'll do the talking here' kind of a look.

"Who are you?"

The marker went for another spin. A-L-W-A-Y-S.

"Always? What does that mean?" Claire demanded. Jake was dumbfounded. He was certainly not pushing the marker, and he was pretty sure that she wasn't either. The board answered.

W-A-T-C-H-I-N-G. *Always watching?* Jake looked over his shoulder and shuffled closer to Claire, who just frowned.

"Is Grandpa still alive?" The marker went to NO first and then shifted to YES. It then rested between the two. "That's not a very clear answer," she complained.

"What is in those lakes?" she countered. The marker spun in tight circles, faster this time, like it was short-circuited.

"Ask it yes or no questions," Jake said, not afraid to admit that the board was scaring the heck out of him.

"Should we go back to the Gem Lakes?"

The marker did not move for quite some time. When it did, it did not go to either yes or no. With each letter the room seemed to get one degree colder. It spelled out N-O-T A-L-O-N-E. N-E-V-E-R A-L-O-N-E.

Claire was not expecting the Ouiji board to side with Jake. So when they awoke the next morning, Claire wanted one final thing from Jake before she agreed to his "with or without you" terms. She wanted him to go with her to Station Bay, so they could climb up to the tracks and put their initials on the train station. It was their summer ritual and she wanted this summer, especially, to be etched in the old wood.

They entered the perfect calm of Station Bay with easy strokes of their paddles. The water was still and peaceful, sheltered from the blustery wind of the open water. The dock had not been maintained in many years and had taken a beating from the weather. It now took on the rustic grey colour of petrified wood. It sagged noticeably in the middle and the front left post had broken away from the frame. Seaweed from the bottom of the lake and bush from the shore threaded through every crack.

Jake threw a loop of rope around a relatively sturdy post and hopped onto the dock. As they stepped on it, water seeped through the spaces between the boards. The train station was up the hill. The path that had worn down to rock many years ago had, surprisingly, not yet been taken over by moss or grass.

As they made their way up the incline, they passed the ramshackle remains of old outboard motor sheds. The cottagers, back in the day, used to haul over their outboard motors in the fall and lock them in sheds by the dock, where they could be easily retrieved the next spring.

Since the road had been put in, the sheds had fallen out of use and had not fared well. They were rotting into the ground.

When Jake and Claire emerged from the cool, shady forest, they stepped directly into the stifling heat of the train tracks. Sweat popped instantly on the back of their necks and their foreheads. They could hear a train chugging far off in the distance. It was impossible to tell if it was on this track or the one that crossed the road farther south. Either way, it seemed like it was miles away.

Jake flipped open his pocketknife. Carving their names on the station was a yearly ritual. Neither he nor Claire had spoken out loud about the fact that was likely the last time he would be doing his.

He could see his name on the paint chipped walls a dozen times already. There were literally hundreds of carvings on the outer and inner walls of the structure.

Claire walked into the station, and immediately found some relief from the heat. There were a few stray logs in one corner, wet with mildew and black with mold. The old iron fireplace, smack in the middle of the room, sat like a lonely soldier manning the fort. The bottom had rusted out and was in a heap below. Claire could just imagine what this place would have been like packed with people in the cold late fall, waiting for a train that could run as much as seven hours late.

She took her pocketknife out (hers was different than Jake's only in the fact that she had a deer carved on the handle, while he had a wolf) and picked a spot on the inside door frame, right by Michael Lucci's admirably carved name. Perhaps next year, she would draw a heart around the names.

Claire stuck her head out and made sure Jake wasn't going to walk in and see her location. He would relentlessly make fun of her for the rest of the day. *Claire and Mikey sitting in a tree, first comes love, then comes marriage, then comes Claire with a baby carriage!*

She had just finished the second leg of her 'R' when she heard the old fireplace begin to rattle. She did not realize what it was until she heard the familiar high-pitched buzz coming off the tracks. The train was definitely on this track and it was closer than they had thought. Much closer.

She dropped the knife and ran out into the bright sunshine. It blinded her for a few seconds but her heart lurched at the dark form near the rail. Jake was down on one knee, fighting off another sword of pain from somewhere deep in his head, and was oblivious to the oncoming danger.

The bloodcurdling shriek that escaped her throat did not sound human and was matched by the desperate whistle of the train that had just rounded the bend and had no hope of stopping.

Claire did not even know she was running towards Jake, her instincts driving her forward as she picked up his dead weight and threw herself sideways, the sharp ballast raking her exposed skin. Claire held Jake tight and pushed her back against the rock on the other side. She had more time than she had realized but not enough to cross the track to safety. She tried to make herself and her brother as skinny as possible. He was still clutching his temples, still trying to rip the pain out.

The earth shook as the train hurtled by, less than five feet away. The noise was unbearable, the screeching of steel wheels on steel track, sparks hopping and jumping beneath the speeding freighter. Claire clamped her eyes shut and waited for a bone-shaking eternity.

A whoosh of wind signalled that the last car had mercifully passed. She cradled her brother's head in her arms, his hair wet and matted. His eyes were open.

"What are you doing?"

Claire started thumping his chest with her fists.

"*What am I doing*," she shrieked, "you almost got killed! That train almost killed you!"

Jake looked like a boxer that had just gone twelve rounds before being knocked out. He was groggy, but coming to steadily. He grabbed his sister's arm. "You *can't* tell Mom and Dad…you *can't!*" If they caught wind of this, the canoe trip was as good as over.

The adrenaline was dropping quickly in Claire's system.

"Forget it Jake, I'm not going there and neither are you. What if this happens again?"

"I just forgot my pill this morning, that's all. I promise it won't happen again…I promise!"

They got up slowly and walked back toward the path. When they got to the dock, they found their father there in Old Reliable, quickly throwing a looped rope over the same post where their canoe was tied.

"Are you two all right? What was that whistle about?"

Claire looked him directly in the eye. "There was a bear on the track Dad. Farther down the way, towards the parking lot. It ran into the bush."

The next night, sitting at one end of the dinner table, Susan Lucknow was not impressed, as was evident in her arched eyebrows and furrowed brow. She would remain quiet, however, until she got Bob alone. He spoke to the children now.

"I want you two to leave in the morning, before the wind picks up."

"What time Dad?" The plan for a canoe trip had been presented, under false pretenses, and accepted much quicker than Jake had expected. They only had to haggle over a few points and the deal was done. Jake had noticed that his father was much more pliable lately and he had no illusions as to the reason. His mother, for the same reason, had become much less so. The sickness had a different effect on everybody.

"Six o'clock. At first light."

The Lucknow brood, especially Claire, looked incredulous. She hadn't expected the plan to get out of the starting gate, never mind the early send-off. The Ouiji board had warned to not go alone. It said nothing about not going at all as Jake had pointed out numerous times throughout the night.

"Dad! The birds aren't even up at six!"

"Tell that to the bloody crow that wakes me up every day."

After dinner, Bob and Jake built a small fire in the metal pit to keep the bugs away. Susan wore a mosquito hat that made her look like something between an alien and a badminton net. Claire wrapped a blanket around herself and sat at her mother's feet.

They had already packed their backpacks, made their sandwiches and filled two canteens with lime-flavoured fruit drink. Their father had snuck in two cans of beans and a tin of canned ham. They had flashlights and waterproof matches. They had sleeping bags, canned soup, a pot, a pan and little metal utensils. They had sunscreen, bug repellant and, of course, the purple pup tent that Mom had bought for Christmas last year. Also from last Christmas was the multi-coloured wool sweater that his mother had made for him, with a goofy looking Rudolph front and centre, red nose in all its glory.

"Mom, I'm not wearing that," Jake had said earlier.

"What's wrong with it?"

Jake did not want to offend his mother. What was wrong with the sweater was that he was at least ten years too old and by his estimation, the wrong sex, to be wearing that sweater anywhere. He chose another route.

"It's summer Mom."

"This is the warmest thing down here! It gets very cool at night. Bring it or don't go." She had said that last sentence through a clenched smile. *Game, set and match.*

The plan, at least the one that they told their parents, was a one-night camping trip on Timber Wolf Lake, which the family had done together several times a year for as long as the kids could remember. They had done everything short of file a flight plan and were now just relaxing on the dock, looking out on the blackened lake which was as smooth as asphalt in the stillness of the night.

Susan produced a bag of marshmallows and the kids quickly hunted down suitable sticks. Jake and Claire had vastly different theories on how a marshmallow should be cooked.

Claire would painstakingly rotate hers well above the heat of the fire, toasting it uniformly until it was a golden brown. It took her fifteen minutes of turning and inspections before she would declare her marshmallow suitable for eating.

Jake, on the other hand, merely thrust his marshmallow directly into the flames, turning it only to make sure that the entire treat was aflame. He would pull the stick out and hold it up like a torch until the flame had formed a bumpy black crust. He would pull off the crust and devour it, putting the remaining goo back into the flame. He could repeat this about three times with one marshmallow, and would be done by the time Claire had turned hers twice.

"Dad, can you tell us a story?" asked Jake. Lately, he wasn't bored anymore by his father's tales, especially the old ones about the lake.

"Sure sport. Which one tonight?"

"How about the Morley brothers?"

His father laughed. "You like that one huh? All right."

It was after the ice melt of 1920. The prized twenty lots had been surveyed and distributed on a first-come, first-serve basis and the new land owners had come to begin the tedious task of hauling over the various materials and tools that would later become the cabins that still stood today.

A trio of brothers—Marvin, Milo, and Martin Morley, in a dangerous combination of testosterone and whiskey, perhaps trying to finish the job before the sun went down, decided to load the large rocks for their would-be-fireplace on top of an already full barge that was to be hauled behind an equally full fishing boat.

The brothers Morley made it halfway across the lake before their sluggish barge cracked down the middle. Witnesses on the shoreline would later recall how all three brothers leapt from the boat to the floundering barge, trying in vain to save what they could.

One by one they started struggling in the icy water, each one too occupied with sinking boulders to remember helping each other. One by one they went under, first Marvin, then Martin, finally Milo. The barge lasted another minute before following them down, dragging the fishing boat with it. There was nothing anybody on shore could do.

Since then, the pile of rocks and rotted wood at the bottom of the lake was known as Morley's Cabin. It had created a man-made reef that was the best fishing on the lake.

Even though the kids had heard this story many times before, they were still listening to their father's version with rapt attention.

"Daddy?" Claire had never asked the question that she finally had the courage to right now.

"Did they just…you know…leave them in there? In the lake I mean."

The mere thought of having swum with skeletons sent shivers down her spine.

"You mean are the Morley's at home?" he chortled. "That depends on who you ask, but, in reality, the RCMP came the next morning and pulled them out."

"Were they…"

"Dead? As doornails. That's what happens when you don't wear your lifejackets and you act like a fool in a boat. I was going to say, your grandfather used to tell me that some time after the accident, people used to see a green glow coming from the middle of the lake. They said it was the Morley brothers coming back to build their cabin right where it fell. In fifty feet of water."

Neither Claire nor Jake could bring themselves to turn around and look at the lake. The full yellow moon reflected in each other's eyes, proof enough that the green glow must be throbbing from the bottom of the lake, the dead Morley brothers settling down for another long, cold night.

"Now get on to bed. You've got an early start tomorrow."

Susan has started tucking Jake in again, and so far he had not objected.

Tonight, the night before her children's first unsupervised canoe trip, she held her warm hand to Jake's clammy forehead. Jake kept his emotions close to his vest. He rarely cried, never discussed his feelings, and barely even liked being hugged. Susan supposed the latter had more to do with his age than his gender, but she didn't mind.

The mere fact that he was letting her tuck him in again spoke volumes on how he was feeling.

Jake must have fallen asleep early tonight, because Claire, from her bunk below, heard her mother whisper her usual prayer for her boy and then leave the room, quietly crying. In moments, Claire pulled a pillow over her head as she heard her brother stifle his own tears, which always came after their mother left the room. She never said anything, so not to embarrass Jake, and she often wondered if the entire cabin cried itself to sleep at night.

PART TWO

Bob Lucknow held the front of the canoe with one hand and passed Jake the backpacks and sleeping bags with the other. He watched Jake carefully, trying to make sure that he was physically up for a trip across the lake. Claire could handle herself, but Bob didn't want her to take too much responsibility for her brother.

Jake, however, looked eager and excited, and Bob hadn't seen that in a long, long time.

"So let's go over the flight plan again."

Jake was uncomfortable lying to his father, but he figured that if he found Grandpa, Dad would forgive him.

"We're going to the far side of Timber Wolf. We'll be camping on the second island in the Bay of Fangs."

"Hmmm, the second fang...good choice. What time will you be home?"

Jake had absolutely no idea how long his quest would take, but he figured not more than the weekend. "We'll be home for Sunday dinner."

Bob Lucknow smiled and passed Claire a small, waterproof container.

"What's this?" she groaned.

The GEM LAKES

"It's my emergency lake kit. Bandages, fishing line, lures, matches. You know...survival stuff," he winked as he gave the canoe a push off the shore. Claire packed the kit away in her backpack.

Claire was battling mixed feelings, scared about lying to her parents, scared about what would happen if Jake had another blackout. The train incident was still fresh in her mind. On the plus side, her brother had promised to take his pills and she trusted that he would. She was also looking forward to some alone time with her brother, without their parents smothering them or watching over their shoulders.

Claire had always loved the outdoors, and she wasn't afraid of some serious paddling. She was the kind of girl who avoided the cheerleading squad like they were infected with bubonic plague.

Fishing was not her cup of tea and only reinforced her opinion that men were a rung lower on the intellectual ladder to get such pleasure out of floating in a boat for hours only to relive it all as soon as they got home.

Nonetheless, she lately always found time to paddle Jake around the lake if he wanted to fish. Although, now that she thought about it, he never seemed to catch anything.

"We'll see you then. Have fun and be careful. Watch out for each other." Bob was looking at Claire when he had said that. *Watch out for your brother.*

It only took an hour for Jake and Claire to paddle across Timber Wolf Lake, in the exact opposite direction of the Bay of Fangs, to the northeast shore. They paddled past the old sign pointing out the way three times before they were able to spot it through overgrown bush. It was a knotted and cracked wooden sign that hung heavily on a tree trunk by a single rusted nail.

"There!" pointed Claire, "On the tree!"

Jake had expected it to take much longer to find the entrance into the Gem Lakes. Finding it so quickly had not given him sufficient time to scare himself out of the idea.

He had also expected to find a portage marker, a triangular sign that named the next lake and distance to it on the sides of the triangle. He had not expected to find the roughly cut board that was nailed across the marker. The sun-baked paint was chipping off in flakes but there was no mistake as to what it read: DANGER—KEEP OUT. The sign seemed to be struggling to stay attached, as if it was waiting for them, saying, *Please hurry, I can't hold on much longer.*

They had to make their way through thick bullrushes to get to shore. Their bare feet sank in the hot mud and flies bit at their ankles. The bullrushes were taller than they were and left tiny cuts on their arms as they pushed them aside.

"Are we having fun yet?" Claire asked.

They put the canoe on shore and tried not to look at the sign. It scared Claire because she did not understand why a forest would be dangerous. Jake was more frightened because he did know.

"It's just to keep little kids out," he said, trying to reassure his sister.

The siblings tied their sleeping bags to their packs, and lifted the canoe over their heads. That probably prevented them from seeing the old sign fall off the tree, splitting in half on the grass below, the ancient, rusted nail unable to hang on for another second.

Perhaps they would have taken that as a sign of things to come and turned back, maybe for a nice campfire in the Bay of Fangs, and then back to Lampshine Lake in time for Sunday dinner. As it was, they moved forward, not knowing what lay ahead of them and, for the time being, not even sure if the knot in their stomachs were being tied by excitement or fear.

About two minutes into the Opal Portage, Jake was beginning to wonder if this little adventure of his was going to get any further than the first lake.

The passage was completely overgrown, a tangle of branches and bush that made carrying the canoe over their heads virtually impossible. It didn't even look like animals had used the trail in ages. *Was this even the trail?*

They had to stop and carry the canoe by the side, and when the bush closed in even further, by the ends, which was awkward and made their arms rubbery. Jake was afraid that if he turned around, he would still be able to see Timber Wolf Lake.

Then there were the bugs. They were getting progressively thicker with each passing step and they had already stopped three times in five minutes to re-apply repellant on their bare arms and necks. They had used a quarter of the bottle already and absolutely reeked.

There was no buzzing or swarming, just a steady, silent attack, which was the most maddening thing of all. You could never tell where they were coming from. In fact, other than the sound of Jake's and Claire's grunting and groaning as they manhandled the canoe through the trees, there was no sound at all.

Claire started whistling, unnerved by the silence. Forests were not typically so quiet. Peaceful, yes, quiet, no. There were always birds singing, frogs croaking, squirrels chirping and clicking, and deer rustling through the bush, cracking branches as they stepped. She found the silence more suffocating than the surrounding trees.

Jake did not notice the quiet as he was too busy dealing with the bugs. He couldn't tell if they were flies, mosquitoes, or those blasted invisible things that his dad called no-see-ums. He did know that they seemed to be taking liberal chunks out of his flesh. He was thankful that they had decided to wear long pants or it would have been completely unbearable.

His arms felt stretched and his shoulders were beginning to burn but he would not be the one to call the first break. He was the man after all. Sickness or not, the embarrassment factor was too much for him to endure. Claire had begun whistling as well, which annoyed him even further. He did not say anything to her. He didn't want to cause a fight already; especially when they were close enough to home that she could turn around and go back without him. In that case, he would have to go with her. The Mad Trapper had warned him not to go alone. So did the Ouiji board. Although he would never say it out loud, he needed Claire, and if he really thought about it, he kind of wanted her with him too. The trapper was right, there were things in life, quite a few things actually, that were better off not faced alone.

"Do you really think we should have let them go alone?" Susan Lucknow asked for the third time in an hour. And that was only the latest hour.

She was furiously scrubbing a breakfast pan with steel wool. Even though it could have been declared clean ten minutes ago and sparkling about two minutes ago, it was now threatening to be proclaimed as glimmering.

Bob watched with mild amusement from the couch, where his attention was divided between a crossword puzzle and the spectacle of his wife scour a hole through the cast-iron pan. If she kept up her current pace, she might break through by mid-afternoon.

"They'll be fine dear. They've been to the Bay of Fangs a hundred times."

"Yes, a hundred times with us. What about Jake? What will Claire do if he has a black out?"

"He has his pills. It's just one night. He'll be okay. Besides, she knows the procedure."

Susan increased her scrubbing speed. Bob wondered if she was scrubbing or just polishing now. "Look honey, camping out is part of growing up. I thought we discussed that we wouldn't treat him like a bed-ridden old man…that we wouldn't hold him back." Bob had stuck to that strategy like a security blanket. It was his game plan, his playbook. Life would continue on as is until the tumour said otherwise.

He had cried the night of the diagnosis but not since. His wife was an emotional eggshell; Claire was still in the denial stage, because in her teenage world, the young were invincible to disease. That was for old people. And Jake, well, he wasn't sure how Jake was handling it. He moved in and out of phases. Tired one week, fine the next, moody one day, happy the next. He sometimes thought that Jake was the one holding them all together.

Bob, of course, felt that was *his* duty. He was the man of the house, the head of the table. He would not allow himself to break down in front of anyone. Someone had to be the rudder on the good ship Lucknow. It would not be, *could not be*, his wife, who, incredibly, was still going to town on the pan. He gave it five minutes for either the pan to disintegrate or her arm to fall off.

With her back turned to him, Bob did not see her eyes overflow, a streak of salty tears roll down her cheek, linger on the corner of her lips and then fall like perfectly formed raindrops to the hardwood floor.

Susan felt like crying all the time. Every minute she was awake, every second of her dreams. It was the hardest not to cry in front of Jake…not to grab him in a bear hug in the hope that she might protect him from anything that came to take him away. She felt so helpless and frustrated that the threat came from the inside, that it wasn't something she could throw herself in front of.

She found herself, at times, seething with jealousy at other parents' healthy kids, which she thought was terrible but she couldn't help it. It's not that she wished the sickness on anybody else, just out of her son. That's all. Was that too much to ask? Jake had said more than once that it wasn't fair. Susan had reeled off the appropriate response that the doctors had given her to memorize; a robotic, non-feeling, science-laced paragraph about how some people's bodies had overactive cells, that it was nothing that they did, blah, blah, blah.

But you know what it comes down to, Susan thought to herself, *it isn't fair. It's not fair to him and it's not fair to me. Why do I have to watch my son die, while everyone else gets to watch theirs live? Why me?*

It sounded selfish, even in her head, but so what? *Tell me...tell me just one thing that's fair about an inoperable tumour*, her mind hissed to nobody in particular. Just...one...thing!

Jake and Claire were standing on the muddy banks of Opal Lake. They had gone up a low hill, where Claire had finally called for a break, and had just come down the other side when the lake appeared through the suddenly thinning trees. Just like that, a half hour of walking, up and over a small bump and there it was, the first of the Gem Lakes.

It was fantastically ordinary. Both the Lucknow children had been on guard for a variety of monsters or wild animals but all they saw was a plain old lake. Both were expecting the portage to take several hours and were now caught off guard at the prospect of actually dipping the canoe in the first of the notorious lakes. It wasn't even that big. They could see the black outline of the trees on the opposite shore. They might be in the second lake within a couple of hours.

"Well, now what?" Claire asked, waving her arms around like an airplane propeller, trying to keep the ever-present insects away. She knew what was next but there was no harm in floating one more chance to turn back.

But Jake was already pushing the canoe toward the water's edge while a halo of flies hovered over his baseball cap. His eyes were scanning the shoreline for the next portage marker. Claire clenched her jaw and picked up the paddles. *Here we go.*

If they thought that making it out of the forest would provide relief from the bugs, they were mistaken. They seemed to come out of the lake itself and as Jake and Claire loaded the canoe with their packs, the swarm descended on them like bloodthirsty birds. The repellent, more than half gone, acted more like an attractant. The hot mud belched disgusting sucking sounds as their feet sank with each step, threatening to hold them in place like quicksand.

"Get in before we're eaten alive!" Jake shouted, swallowing three or four bugs in the process. Claire took her spot in the back and pushed off the muck of the shore.

Usually water appears to be blue. The reflection of the sky on a clear lake will make it a light or dark blue, depending on the cloud cover. This lake, however, seemed to take its colour from the bottom, which was clearly very muddy. While paddling on Lampshine or even Timber Wolf, Jake was able to see right to the bottom, even able to catch a glimpse of the occasional fish passing underneath. But, on Opal Lake, it was a murky stew that seemed to get darker with each stroke of the paddle.

The water wasn't the only thing dark. The trees on the opposite shore were not getting any greener either. They had appeared black from the portage but they had only been able to see the outline. They were about halfway across the lake now and they still seemed shadow-like, almost as if the light was dissolving when it hit them.

Out on the lake, the bugs had mostly backed off. Jake was once again at the bow of the canoe, but this time it was not due to fatigue. While he had always preferred to "steer" the canoe from the back, he now wanted to be the first one to see whatever trouble they were getting into. The Mad Trapper had told him to grow eyes in the back of his head, and while that sounded like a bit much, he wanted to spot any danger before it spotted them.

On that note, Jake turned his attention to a large weed bed on their right-hand side. A little farther back, he thought he had noticed movement amongst the reeds, but now he was sure. Was it a bear? Maybe it was a giant snake, sensing movement in the lake for the first time in a long time.

The answer popped out of the reeds a moment later; a duck. Jake did a double take. It was a *very* large duck—gigantic actually. It looked more like a goose but by its metallic green head, Jake knew it was a mallard. Two more ducks followed out of the camouflage of the reed bed—then three more, then six. They were all the same size, their heads bigger than softballs and still pouring out of the cover. There were at least twenty of them and they seemed to be getting riled up. They were letting out sharp, quick quacks. A warning? Maybe a battle cry?

Claire saw them too. "Do ducks have teeth?" she whispered, apparently certain that they were under imminent attack.

Jake did not think so but he didn't want to find out the hard way. The ducks scuttled back and forth, getting louder by the second but sticking close to their home base. They were waiting…waiting to see how close these strangers were going to come.

Jake was a little bit frightened, as people usually are with things they haven't seen before, but the beauty of the birds also mesmerized him. He had never seen this many males in one group. He did not see one female, whose plain-Jane-brown-and-white plumage would have stuck out like a sore thumb against the colours of the males. Their green heads and orange beaks were vibrant, like they had been freshly painted on. Their wings were a splash of cobalt blue against a canvas of snow white feathers. He wished he had taken a camera but he was not here to sightsee. Still…

"Let's get a little closer," he said, "Just a little."

Claire, too, was fascinated by the sheer size of the ducks and she pointed the canoe just slightly towards them. That was a mistake.

Obviously taking the change of direction as an act of aggression, the ducks roared from the water in an explosion of powerful wings and flying feathers, the scattered quacking now a high-pitched screeching, like nails across a chalkboard.

Jake and Claire screamed.

"Paddle! Paddle! Paddle!" Jake yelled.

The freak ducks were on them in no time, taking turns swooping down and battering them with their huge wings, pecking at them with their bright orange beaks. Claire started waving her paddle at the frenzied attackers, making contact only once with a solid thump, sending one of the oversized waterfowl spinning head first into the lake.

Jake had pulled his hat down low and was bearing down on the paddle. He was hoping that under the cover of trees, the ducks would retreat. Unfortunately, with Claire's paddle engaged in battle, he couldn't keep a straight course. "Help me paddle! We've got to get to the trees!"

Claire reluctantly returned her weapon to the water and instantly doubled their pace. There was no greater motivator for speed than fear.

The Lucknows' panic seemed to make the ducks go even crazier and they were now in a blind rage. They started dive-bombing the canoe with such fury that they would sometimes smash into each other instead, while others would miss the canoe completely and hit the water so hard that it knocked them out.

When they did make contact, it felt like being hit with a basketball launched from a slingshot, like a game of dodgeball gone very bad.

Jake and Claire were not far from shore and fear and the adrenaline that came with it fuelled their muscles beyond what they thought they had in them. Finally, after what seemed like an hour, but what was in reality only a few minutes, the canoe scraped the muddy bottom of the north shore. They scrambled out of the canoe and raced towards the trees.

Jake's prayers were answered. The ducks stopped dead as soon as they hit the tree line. They all just fell from the air, seemingly exhausted and quite unwilling to follow them onto land. They swam away, back towards the reeds, almost like nothing had happened.

With their hearts trying to beat out of their chests, Jake and Claire sat down on a rock, looking out on Opal Lake in bewildered silence. The map had not said anything about the freak ducks. There were no strange symbols or markings until after the next lake. Perhaps the Mad Trapper didn't consider the massive mallards particularly noteworthy. The Lucknow children were wondering with dread what he did.

It took them three hours to find the portage marker into Emerald Lake. The triangular wooden sign looked petrified it was so old, but it seemed to be holding together well otherwise. They had pulled ashore on a heavily treed part of the shore during their hasty escape from the crazed ducks and had not been lucky enough to chance upon the next portage. It had taken them one of the three hours just to get up enough courage to get back in the canoe and patrol the shore for the marker.

They had kept one eye on the trees and the other on the ducks, which had returned to the cover of the reeds and didn't seem the least bit interested in them anymore.

The marker had been only slightly easier to spot this time, hanging under a great umbrella of branches, mostly protected from the ravages of weather, the black letters were still legible; Emerald Lake, 4 km.

On the map, four kilometres looked like a hop, skip, and a jump into the next lake. The distance on paper was a few centimetres at most. The *actual* distance, when you considered the rocky hills and dense trees was never-ending. Mercifully, the bug situation could now be downgraded to tolerable. The insects had been left to breed in the murky muck that was Opal Lake, surely the source of every mosquito and black fly on the planet.

At their current pace, Jake seriously doubted that they would get much farther before they would have to start scouting out campsites for the night. Carrying the canoe over their heads was beginning to wear on their backs. They found that if they wore their life jackets while they walked, they could rest the canoe on their padded shoulders, making it much easier on their spines. Without much argument, they made a goal to reach the next portage marker and then quit for the day.

The GEM LAKES

Jake had not told Claire about the bear caves. As they stood at the first rocky embankment, the beginning of which would be the gauntlet of caverns and caves, mostly occupied by cantankerous, no doubt oversized, hopefully-not-hungry brown bears, Jake wondered if it was such a good thing to spring this information on her at the last moment.

The option, having it fester in her mind for a few days as it did in his, would have resulted in some serious fleeing consideration. The Mad Trapper's words, "*You'll scare yourself out of those lakes before you even lay eyes on them,*" rang true. Jake had been dreading this early part of the journey more than any other. He was not a big fan of bears.

He surveyed the obstacle in front of them. Carrying the canoe, they could not possibly climb *over* the steep rocks as Jake had hoped. Instead, they would have to go right between the two massive walls of moss-covered granite, the "path" itself being a track of stones and shattered rock.

It would be a very slow and awkward walk, in the very place that they needed to be quick and agile.

Cracks and fissures connected the openings of the caves, which were dark and impossible to see into. Their only real hope was that the bears were not at home. Jake would not have bet a single penny on that though.

Claire was getting impatient. "What are we waiting for? Christmas?"

Jake winced. She had apparently inherited their mother's dripping sarcasm. He picked up his pack, "All right, let's go. But let's be quiet, all right?"

Claire saw the red flags right away. To her, the comment might as well have been a wailing, flashing siren screaming, "*Trouble ahead, trouble ahead!*"

"Be quiet? Why?" she asked with equal parts suspicion and dread.

Jake would continue to be as vague as possible. "We don't know what's in these caves."

"Caves? They just look like breaks in the rock to me. What do you mean caves? Are you keeping something from me?"

No Claire, he wanted to say, *It's actually a freakin' hotel of cranky bears that are probably bigger than Cadillacs. What's a Cadillac, you ask? It's a car...a very big car. I'm sure their claws are ridiculously long too. Their fangs? Don't get me started on their fangs...*

"They're caves. Bear caves. Be quiet and they won't hear us!" Jake, for just the briefest of moments, actually enjoyed the look of shock in his older sister's eyes...just for a moment. At least she was quiet, too scared to do anything but follow directions. "Just walk as quick as you can over the rocks and look ahead. Don't look into the caves. Don't worry, it's not that far." That didn't even sound reassuring to Jake. As he looked ahead, the length appeared to be about half a football field. Not so long if you were the Winnipeg Blue Bombers, but fairly lengthy for two kids with a canoe and a bear infestation on their hands.

There was nothing to do but start walking. They couldn't do anything about the bears until they actually saw one.

Walking on the rocks, some the size of basketballs, other the size of oranges, proved even more difficult than they had thought. They were forced to move in slow motion to prevent their ankles from rolling or their feet getting caught. Jake could not think of a worse spot on the planet to break a leg.

The tip of the canoe cut off the top half of Jake's vision, and both sides were blinded, making it the most unnerving walk of his life. The feeling of not knowing what was behind them was terrible. He wanted more than anything to drop the canoe and turn around but stopping at this point was out of the question.

Claire, who was carrying the back of the canoe, had this feeling multiplied by ten. The caves were on either side...the bears were on either side, but she could not see on either side! It did not make sense to her. She knew he was passionate about this trip but this was ridiculous. Jake was pushing on when he should be turning around.

She had almost had enough and if she had even a grain of courage to turn around and face those ducks alone, she would have. Now, they needed each other. If the trail didn't start getting easier, they were going to have a serious problem. Both needed the other to face the lakes, but they would soon want to head in opposite directions. The result of that would be their standing still, and that was not an option; not with things that seemed ready to jump out of the forest at any moment.

Jake's spine was beginning to feel like jelly by the time he realized that he was walking on dirt. He had been so focused on getting through the rocks that he didn't even notice he was past them. He lifted the canoe over his head and dared a glance over his shoulder. The caves were behind him with not a bear in sight. For some reason that he could not explain, he started laughing. Claire turned around and she started laughing as well. They had made it. Their imaginations had managed to scare them half to death.

They rested the canoe on the ground and high-fived each other like they had just teamed up for the winning goal in the Stanley Cup Final. It would have been the most short-lived celebration in NHL history, because as they turned around they came face-to-face with the twenty-five hundred pound bull moose that was blocking their path only a few metres away, snorting and grunting in a most unpleasant manner.

The moose would surely have blocked out the sun if it had wandered in front of it. Its back leg was kicking up dirt, digging a hole faster than a bulldozer, with hooves that could have doubled as end tables. Its head was three times bigger than the one mounted on the Mad Trapper's wall with a set of antlers so mammoth that you could very likely hang a thousand hats from it. It was a rack that was now pointed down, directly at the Lucknow siblings.

There was only one thing to do and only one place to do it. Without a thought for bears or broken legs, Jake and Claire turned around and ran back through the caves, leaving the canoe where they had dropped it. Seeing them run, the moose charged.

The hulking moose was having serious trouble with the rocks, which infuriated him even more. Wet steam blew from its nostrils as it bellowed and honked, while the Lucknows, who had stepped so carefully through the rocks the first time, now ran through it like Olympic sprinters. A broken ankle would be the least of their problems.

The storming moose was making more noise than a fireworks show at a jackhammer convention. As a result, the slumbering bears were waking up and swarming out of the caves.

The bears could be classified as small only in comparison to the behemoth bull. Their attention was mostly drawn directly to Mr. Moose…mostly, not all. A few, who had seen moose in the forest many times, were far more interested in the two-legged animals running farther on in the same direction. Rule number one in encountering a bear; don't turn your back and run, they tend to chase. And chase they did.

When Jake quickly looked back to see how close the moose was to running him down, he was shocked to see that he had developed a new problem. Un-freaking-believable! Bears! The moose was bogged down in a gang of big brown bears, none too happy about being woken up from their nap. In its place were three other bears, rumbling after them with powerful strides.

"Tree! Go for the tree!" was all he had time to get out. Claire went for one tree, Jake another and both tried to shimmy themselves up the trunk to reach a branch. Jake grabbed one for dear life and pulled. He got up on the first branch and didn't stop climbing until he ran out of tree.

He caught his breath, looked down and saw Claire lying on the ground, the bears surrounding her in a tight circle, lumbering around and around, examining their new prize. Jake tightened his grip on the branch. She was faking dead, a trick their dad had told them a long time ago. At least, he hoped she was faking.

The GEM LAKES

Claire was never good at climbing trees and just because her life was on the line, she wasn't about to wager that it would suddenly come to her. Her father had once told her that you could play dead for a certain kind of bear and they would just leave you alone. She just couldn't remember if it was a brown or a black bear. She figured her odds were zero with the tree and fifty-fifty with the fake death. She dropped to the ground, three feet from the nearest climbable tree.

The bears ignored Jake, even though they could have been up his tree in seconds. Jake remembered, now that the hysteria of the chase was over, that climbing is second nature to bears. He had trapped himself at the top of the tree with nowhere to go but down. Claire remained utterly still as the bulky bears sniffed her and pushed at her with their snouts. She could feel their damp, stale breath on her skin and tried hard to breathe only from the corner of her mouth. It had just come to her—it was grizzly bears you could fake dead for. Black bears, you were supposed to make yourself large and loud and they were supposed to run away. She had a feeling that if she stood up and spread her arms and yelled in this crowd, it would be the last thing she ever did.

Facedown, she opened one eye slightly and saw the tremendous foot of one of the animals only inches from her nose. The fur was a cinnamon brown and the five claws curved out—each as long as a butcher knife. If the bears wanted to, they could easily slice her into enough pieces for all of them to share an unexpected snack.

Up in the tree, Jake was frantically trying to come up with a distraction. The bears were panting, taking long swipes at each other over his fallen sister. They were woofing and whining, jostling for the best body part to sink their teeth into.

Jake untied one of his shoes and held it over his head, a feeble weapon for this particular situation, but the only thing he had to work with. He was aiming for the brown muzzle of the biggest of the three bruins, hoping that if he turned and ran then his friends would follow suit.

Jake took careful aim and let the shoe fly. Unfortunately, throwing shoes is not the same as throwing baseballs, especially from the awkward position of a tree limb. The shoe sailed through the air harmlessly and landed under a bush. He quickly untied the other shoe and took aim again.

The second shoe missed the bears completely and bounced off a nearby stump. Jake's heart lurched. He would have to drop from the tree and use himself as a distraction. He was out of options.

One of the bears looked up from Claire and wandered over to the second shoe. But it was not the shoe itself that interested the hungry bear. When the shoe had hit the rotted stump, a stream of red ants poured out from the broken top and flowed over the side. The bear let out a woof of delight and started feasting on the riled ants, prompting his two compatriots to look up and hustle over to the new found insect buffet. The big one roared with jealousy (Claire thought it was her last moment on earth) and tore across the forest floor, knocking the first one completely over. The two rolled and grappled while the third strode up behind them and helped himself.

Emerald Lake, shimmering like smooth green glass, was encircled by a forest of birch trees, their salt-and-pepper trunks reflecting in the polished surface of the water. It was as mesmerizing as it was relieving to be standing at the base of the lake, especially after the close encounter with the burly bears. At first Jake and Claire were afraid that it was glass and thought the surface might crack if they pushed the canoe onto it. Of course, it didn't, but it barely made a ripple either. "C'mon, let's push off before dark."

Jake was in no mood to hang around, not after watching his sister being considered for dinner. Jake had descended shoeless out of the tree, pulled Claire up from the ground and had hastily grabbed both of his wayward footwear. The army of ants had held the attention of the bears, even as Jake had tiptoed near enough to retrieve the shoe closest to the stump. They had then slowly backed up towards the caves where the rampaging moose had managed to battle the bears back into the bush. This time, they did climb over, just in case, and scurried over the top of the bears' housing. When they stepped off the other side, the canoe sat unharmed, right where they had left it.

As it was now, they figured they had just enough daylight left to get to the Sapphire Portage and set up a camp for the night. Emerald Lake was a small lake. It wouldn't take long to cross it...he hoped.

Indeed it should not have taken but twenty minutes to cross the jade water, but the surface was distracting. It was the most beautiful thing that either Jake or Claire had seen in nature. The water swirled in slow motion as they dipped their paddles into the surface. Green teardrops of water rolled down the blade of the paddles and dropped uniformly back into the lake. It was hypnotizing. So much so, in fact, that when the tip of the birch bark canoe bumped into the sandy shore, it startled them both. They had somehow plunked themselves right under the next portage marker. Sapphire Lake, 1 km. The downside was that the twenty-minute trip had somehow eaten up three-and-a-half hours and dusk was about to give way to night.

It was at this exact minute that Claire realized how far she was from Lampshine Lake, her parents, and a roof over her head. She began to panic.

Jake could not understand how such a short distance could have taken such a long time to cover. He was going to ask Claire if he had had another blackout but as he turned around he realized that she wasn't well.

"Claire, what's wrong?"

She was shaking violently, her eyes scanning the forest, blinking like a camera shudder.

Jake grabbed her shoulders and shook her for a moment until she snapped out of it. Tears rolled down her cheeks in a steady stream. "I can't sleep out here. How are we going to sleep out here?

Bears...bears...what if they come back and what else? What else is out here?"

Jake looked at her dumbfounded. She was right. He had been trying to think so far ahead, he forgot to consider getting through the night. Neither of them had been out alone, especially three lakes behind their own, and in an area where every animal seemed to have an attitude problem. "Let's get the tent up. Now!"

The purple two-man pup tent went up in three minutes flat, with still a few moments of light left in the day. They set about collecting wood for a fire but the approaching darkness was making it hard to see. They met back in front of the tent with an armful of branches and twigs. They pulled some grass from the ground and set it under a small pile of the wood. The green grass smoked but didn't catch. Jake had to hold the match right under the smallest, thinnest twig to get it going. Eventually it caught, and all of a sudden, they had fire.

Claire retreated to the tent and zipped the screen down. "You're doing great Jake. Good fire. Excellent fire."

The fire was warming Jake's face and he smiled from the side of his mouth. Claire's voice was still shaking. He looked over for his flashlight but decided to keep it off. He would need to conserve the batteries. The fire was throwing his shadow over the tent, making him look like one of the oversized bears they had seen earlier. He stopped looking at it because it was starting to creep him out.

The fire had a voracious appetite and had soon consumed his entire pile of branches. He realized he would need a few stumps or logs if he could find any, or he'd be out here all night feeding twigs to the fire.

He looked back into the tent and noticed that Claire had passed out asleep. He didn't blame her. He hoped that the bears wouldn't chase her in her dreams. He reached for the flashlight and headed for the edge of the woods. Forget the batteries, he wasn't going in the forest at night without a light!

As he hit the 'on' button on the flashlight, he thought he saw a blur where the beam of light cut through the dark. Something moved behind a tree. He shut the light off and ran back towards the tent, hurdled the wood-deprived fire and whipped the zipper upwards. He jumped in and landed right on top of his slumbering sister. Claire, whose nerves could not have been more frazzled, jumped up screaming.

Jake had to clamp her mouth with his hand. "Sshhhh! Don't say a word!"

They froze in a position that would be awkward even for a game of Twister. They listened hard, hearing only the amplified chirping of thousands of crickets and the dying fire gasping for more fuel. They heard a bullfrog croak every twenty-two seconds, and yes, they counted. They heard a fish jump from somewhere on the lake, and then they heard the talking. Human talking. It was more like mumbling at first, but then a rushed ranting. Two voices first, then two more, talking in a hushed super fast frenzy so that Jake and Claire could not understand a single word. Maybe it wasn't human at all, they thought.

Jake realized that they needed to take a more defensive position, so they crouched on either side of the door and listened some more, absolutely petrified.

The fire had been reduced to embers and was throwing a minimal amount of light. Even so, Jake could see dark shapes moving quickly between the trees, faster than a human could ever move. *This trip*, he thought, *has been a serious mistake.*

"They're scared," A voice said quietly beside Jake. It took him a moment to realize it was Claire's. "They're more scared of us than we are of them."

"I doubt that," he whispered back. The voices were becoming more hurried, almost panicked. Jake was close to joining them.

"No, listen!"

The voices became so rushed that they could not distinguish one voice from the others. Then nothing...like they had vanished into thin air.

"They're gone," Claire announced.

"How do you know? Maybe they're just watching us."

Claire frowned as she peeked out the tent doors. "Why'd you have to say that? How am I supposed to sleep?"

Sleep did come eventually, but not until the morning sun poked above the horizon in the very early morning. The comforting light tugged their eyelids closed for the first time in twenty-four hours. They would not awaken until mid-afternoon, by then a full day behind schedule.

"It's a little choppy," Jake observed.

That was an understatement. White caps rose furiously from the far shore, gathered violent momentum across the open water and crashed brutally into the rocky shore at their feet. The canoe would become nothing more than a floating coffin if they set it in that thrashing water.

"We'll have to wait it out...maybe it will calm down tonight."

Claire was more than a little concerned about the current pace of the trip. They were due back in mere hours.

They had wasted the day sleeping, the afternoon sun melting away the fears from the previous night. A couple of hours later, they had written off the noises and talking as their overactive imaginations.

The wind died down somewhere between four o'clock and five, as it often does in the late afternoon in lake country, and Jake and Claire wasted no time getting the canoe back into the water. Sapphire Lake, as might have been expected, was a brilliant blue, free of any algae or seaweed that tinged most of the water they had seen. Completely surrounded by thick jack pines, with their rough cover of shingled bark and their tall, slightly leaning trunks, Sapphire seemed like an "old" forest.

As they paddled closer to the opposite shore, Jake was having a difficult time picking out a spot to set the tent up. The jack pines did not look like they were willing to share a common ground.

The **GEM LAKES**

There was one bald patch of rock tucked in a little bay. If they could pitch the tent there, they wouldn't have to worry about noises in the forest. That would allow them get to sleep and to get up early.

Sunday dinner sat untouched on the kitchen table, the cold ham became colder, the fresh buns grew crustier and the gravy for the mashed potatoes formed a congealed jelly.

Bob Lucknow anxiously picked at a chicken wing while Susan stood at the back door, arms crossed, ready to unleash a mother's wrath at any moment.

She had been guarding the door for two hours and fourteen minutes. As the second hand on her wristwatch ticked past the twelve to make it an even fifteen minutes she turned around to her husband, "Go get the neighbours and another canoe."

All the families on Lampshine Lake had known each other for generations, and rarely did a Friday or Saturday night go by where one or two or five of the families might pick up and set off down the well-worn sand path for happy hour at the various neighbours. Claire liked to refer to it as 'happy *hours*' because her parents would be gone for at least three on any given afternoon. The lake would come alive with the sound of raucous laughter, singing and games. The clink of a three-point ringer in horseshoes would surely be followed by the whoops of delight from the winning team, not to mention the groans of the opposition.

But other than those few hours a week, the cottagers generally kept to themselves. The main attraction of the serene and secluded lake was peace and quiet after all, not socializing. In the same breath, if somebody ever got into trouble, like the time when Mr. Washburn of Lot Thirteen went missing for six hours on a blazing hot day four years ago, the entire lake community would offer their full resources and support. Mr. Washburn had knocked himself senseless while cutting trees in the back bush for firewood. He had taken the brunt of a misdirected tree trunk right between the eyes. Luckily for him, the wood had rotted halfway up, softening the blow. Nevertheless, it opened him up for twenty-two homemade stitches courtesy of Dr. Jergenson. That and a shot of bourbon, and he declared himself as good as new.

It was after that incident that the cottagers came up with the Horn of Trouble. It was an old, hollowed out animal bone that sat in a simple wooden box that was attached to a prominent tree in the front of Lot Ten. It was for emergencies only. Not the "we ran out of pancake syrup again" kind of emergency, or even the "boat motor's on fire again" kind of emergency. It was strictly for life and death. If the horns chilling sound was heard, you could be sure that something was very, very wrong.

In fact, when Bob Lucknow sounded the horn an hour ago, it was the first time it had been heard on the lake. Its terrible sound cut a swath through the peaceful night, no doubt dropping a few hearts into a few stomachs.

Bob Lucknow surveyed the small crowd that had gathered near his back porch. A lump formed in his throat at the thought of the search crew that had volunteered instantly and without question. The brave front was in full effect and encouraging words were being bandied about. "They're probably sitting on those islands havin' a grand ol' time." But the words were wavering. He saw concern etched in every single face and then there were the eyes. The eyes gave everybody away. There was worry and unease as sure as sugar.

A nagging thought kept pushing its way into Bob's brain and he pushed it back each time with greater authority. The sun was plummeting into the horizon, a wave of pink washed over the yard. It was time to move.

The tiny army of searchers quickly divided themselves into groups of two and made their way to the edge of Timber Wolf Lake, the largest of the lakes in the area. They were outfitted with flashlights and paddles and apprehension.

The GEM LAKES

Bob and Susan headed straight for the Bay of Fangs, and even though it is on the opposite shore, they made good time on the seamless evening water.

The 'second fang' refers to the second of five islands that you encounter at the entrance of the bay. It is the largest and flattest, making it by far the most popular choice for camping. On this night, however, the Lucknows couldn't find any sign that anyone has been camping on it in weeks. There was no blackened campfire pit, no flattened grass where a tent could have been pitched, and no telltale signs of a canoe landing.

The Lucknows left the search of the other 'fangs' to the McLinktoks, from Lot One and made their way along Timber Wolf's north shore.

Meanwhile, Tucker Smith and his eldest son Tucker Jr. checked out Flagpole Bay, aptly named because the thin trees that were found there were straight as arrows and several had indeed been cut down and used as cottage flagpoles back on Lampshine. If the rigid trees had seen anything, they weren't giving it up.

The serene bay was also quite swampy, and Tucker had to carefully lift lily pads to see if there was anything underneath. He hoped beyond hope that he did not find anything, especially with his son in the front of the canoe. Nobody needed that kind of memory.

"Where could they be? We should be checking the other islands!" Susan fretted from the front of the canoe. Her nerves were already frayed and threatening to unravel completely. If they didn't find them by dark...

Bob shook his head and paddled harder to the northeast corner. He knew these lakes like the back of his hand, and knew for certain that the second fang was the only fang worth camping on. The others were too rocky, too steep, too tree infested. He had a nagging suspicion that his children may have stumbled on the one place he really hoped they hadn't.

The sun threw one last length of light across the water, illuminating the nest of bullrushes. They stood straight and tall, unwavering in the eerie stillness, like sentries guarding an ancient palace…or a terrible prison. It was because of the light that they noticed a depression in the bullrushes. There could be no doubt that a canoe had been dragged onto shore not too long ago.

"Look at that sign Bob," Susan pointed to the rotted, broken sign that had settled sideways on the grass. "I've never seen that sign before. Danger? Who would put that up? You don't think they went in there, do you?"

Bob did indeed think the kids had gone back there. Susan had not seen the warning before, even in fifteen years of marriage, because Bob had never taken her to this side of the lake. There was a reason for that.

They must have been staring at the bullrushes for longer than they had realized, because soon the five other canoes surrounded theirs, bobbing chunks of light giving away the company of flashlights. The sun had sunk behind the trees without announcement and the Lucknows had not noticed. They could do no more under the smothering night sky, soon to be blacker than an oil spill until the moon came up, and without the comforting blanket of clouds to prevent the temperature from dropping.

Jake and Claire paddled on. They would have to find that clearing before it got dark.

They had almost made shore when the bottom of the canoe scraped something, lifted the canoe slightly and stopped dead. Jake frowned and peered over the side. It was deadwood. They had rode right up on it.

They paddled backwards with no success. Jake tried pushing off the log with his paddle but stopped when he almost flipped them over.

"We'll have to get out and lift it off," he announced.

"Well get on with it then," Claire grinned.

Jake gave her a look that wiped the smile off her face. Claire rolled up her pants to her knees and stepped out the back of the canoe only to sink down to her belly button. "Aarrgh!" That made Jake smile, and he went to work trying to shake them loose.

The deadwood was covered in green slime and was disgusting to touch. He pulled on it.

"Can you push the canoe?" he asked, turning around to instruct his sister.

Jake stopped and stared, his mouth dropping open. A turtle, an outrageously big turtle, had surfaced behind Claire. He tried to scream a warning but fear and disbelief caught in his throat.

The look on Jake's face was more than enough to let Claire know that there was something disagreeable going on behind her. She looked back over her shoulder and faced what she took to be a dinosaur. It was huge, sickly green with a hideous face and a terribly hooked beak. Claire's shoulders and knees both turned to jello.

The ancient reptile took Jake's paddle squarely on top of its head. It pulled back instinctively, and Jake took that short opportunity to grab Claire by her arms and pull her towards the shore. They had to climb over the deadwood to make it to safety, and when they looked back, the turtle had disappeared, but not for long. It emerged again, this time faster, and sent their canoe flying to the side, breaking the deadwood into pieces in the process. It lunged out of the water and for the first time the kids saw the turtle's claws, any one of which was long and sharp enough to shred them in half. The kids ran as the giant snapper reared its head back with its mouth wide open, like it was trying to scream. A ghastly hissing sound escaped instead. It dropped down and slipped back into Sapphire Lake.

They stared at the lake. There was not a ripple on it. They turned to each other as if to say "Did you see that?" but there was no need for words.

One of their uncles had been down to Lampshine several years ago and had thought it a good idea to go skinny-dipping after dinner. Well, the snapper that lived under the Lucknow dock took a dollar-sized chunk out of his bare butt, sending him screaming up the path towards the cabin. Unfortunately, Uncle Ira had not stopped to grab his towel in his haste to leave the scene. That had not been a pleasant sight.

If the turtle that they had just seen had gotten hold of their father's favourite brother, well, there might not have been much left of him. Jake remembered another thing that the Mad Trapper had told him, "*Be mindful at all times.*"

He turned to Claire and, thinking of the train track incident, winked at her, "I guess we're even now."

The fire had sputtered green smoke for the first hour after they had lit it—the result of the long grass and leafy saplings that they had been feeding it. After finding and kicking apart a partially decomposed tree, the fire was now doing a slow burn. While it was barely throwing any heat, it was quickly losing its effectiveness as a light source as well. It was the lack of light that bothered Claire most.

In the brightness of day-time, the forest was one of Claire's favourite places. She loved the colourful wildflowers, the smell of pine and the clean air off the lake. She liked to feed chipmunks and even the occasional fox who would sometimes come right up to the cabin's back door for after dinner scraps.

By night, however, the forest was terrifying to her. Her own imagination was by far her worst enemy. The same sounds that she barely noticed in the day were amplified and in stereo after dark.

A deer walking through the woods, snapping branches with each step, sounded more like a hefty grizzly bear crashing towards her at full speed. Or who was to say that the small squirrel she thought she was hearing wasn't actually a hungry bobcat, hunting for some easy prey?

And now it was like her imagination had become real. These Gem Lake animals were huge. The snapping turtle was just the latest example that these woods weren't anything like what she was used to.

The GEM LAKES

Jake had fallen asleep by the small fire, curled up in a ball in his sleeping bag. Claire was sitting on the opposite side of the flames, her back against a wall of rock and her knees pulled up to her chest. She wrapped herself tighter in her own sleeping bag, staring at her slumbering brother. She was shaking, although from fear or cold she could not tell.

She turned her flashlight on, making sure the beam of light didn't touch Jake's face. She had waited until he fell asleep to switch the light on, as she had the previous night, because he would scold her for wasting batteries. Indeed, the beam that had been so strong and penetrating at the beginning of the trip was now fading fast. It was a sickly yellow light that was quickly choked off by the blackness of the night.

A good-sized Great Horned Owl could easily make out Claire Lucknow's flashlight flickering. It could see her *will* it to stay on and then the light flicker twice more before it died out for good. She quickly picked herself up off the ground and prodded her brother until he awoke from his sleep. Together, they retreated to the relative safety of the tent.

There was someone else joining them tonight. Even the owl could barely see him but it *heard* him below. A man has spotted the Lucknow camp and has stopped to take a look. As the last gasp of light from Claire's flashlight was extinguished, the man moved forward. The movement was enough to provoke the horned bird to flight. The darkness seemed to harden into an impenetrable veil and it is not certain which direction the visitor had gone.

Bob and Susan awoke from the same dream in which they were falling down a bottomless shaft with their arms tied, smacking and thumping against the sides as they fell, absolutely helpless to stop themselves. They were splayed over the living room furniture, she on the couch, and he in the rocking chair, wearing the same clothes that they had put on yesterday morning. Susan woke first, to an actual thumping sound in the distance. She pushed herself off the couch and made her way to the kitchen window that overlooked the lake.

Two helicopters hovered over the front water like massive black vultures, their blades causing a small windstorm, blowing sand and dirt in every direction. Below them, twelve motorized zodiac rafts were headed towards shore, filled with enough uniformed men to invade a small country.

Last night, they had used Dr. Jergenson's satellite phone to call the Park Ranger and Natural Resources for help. If this was Natural Resources, no wonder they had experienced budget problems last year.

Bob was standing silently behind her. She saw his reflection in the window. "They've all got machine guns. What's in those lakes Bob?"

The call from a frantic Susan Lucknow late the previous evening to the provincial Natural Recourses Department was instantly rerouted to the Department of National Defense. It was a call that Major Duncan Shocklot had not expected to receive in his lifetime. After being promoted to Major and being put in charge of a special unit involving National Safety and Security, he had been briefed on a number of matters that the average Canadian citizen would never even know about, even though those matters may pertain to their very own backyard.

One of those files that landed on his desk was a thick dossier wrapped in CLASSIFIED seals. It contained the long and calamitous history of the Gem Lakes.

It was the only part of North America that remained uncharted. The file was filled with incidents dating back to the Gold Rush era, when the interior of Canada offered a less arduous option than the dangerous journey to the Klondike. Prospectors would hire bush pilots to take them to the north in search of a golden vein of minerals that would make them instantly rich.

The GEM LAKES

There were fifteen incidents on file that noted bush planes going down over the Gem Lakes. Thirty-five people and twelve planes were never recovered. Before that, the Royal Canadian Mounted Police took several complaints of entire Indian hunting bands not returning from the lakes. Indian legend stated that a great cat roamed the lakes and had an appetite for flesh. They called it the *joaquin* and it became so feared that it forced the migration of three different tribes.

Joaquin or not, the Gem Lake Magnetic Field, as it was referred to in the file, was the result of the earth's magnetic fields reversing in the early 1900s. This happens very infrequently, perhaps every one million years. The previous one was estimated to have been seven hundred thousand years earlier.

The sun also had a magnetic field, and when the poles of *that* field reversed, every eleven years like clockwork, then the iron plate that sat under the Gem Lakes turned into a schizophrenic hotplate. Because of the earth flip, the iron plate was already reacting like nowhere else on the planet. When the sun flipped as well, it became 'supercharged' and the result was deformations in animal and plant species among other things.

The sun had daily eruptions, and sent off more solar flares, sending powerful streams of supercharged particles towards earth. It was these blasts that were visible as breathtaking auroras in the night sky and were the exact reason why no communications or electrical systems would function over or on the lakes. Planes and helicopters could not fly over it and it wreaked havoc with electronic weapons.

The government, of course, could have put up barbed-wire fencing or No Trespassing signs but those were just invitations to thrill-seekers and curious types. This area was so isolated they didn't have to worry much. The legends and stories of the *joaquin* were enough to keep the small population of cottager's away...until now.

As the major tramped up the path towards the yellow cabin he steeled himself for a messy confrontation with the Lucknow parents. He would not be sending his men in until he could be certain that the area was secure and that was not likely to go over well. It would be a sad week for them all because, in his mind, the Lucknow children wouldn't survive the week.

Jake and Claire ate lunch on the top of a ridge that overlooked a stunning view of miles and miles of frontier forest. A small meadow of tall grass and wild flowers was the only break between the forest and the ridge.

They basked in the sun and shared a can of tinned ham. About halfway through, Claire stopped in mid-bite and pointed down toward the meadow. A cow moose had wandered into the opening and was chewing on the tall blades of grass. The animal was huge. It was not nearly as big as the bull that they had clashed with at the bear caves, but nonetheless huge.

Jake and Claire watched wide-eyed as the moose munched. The cow looked like she didn't have a care in the world.

It was then that Jake first spotted the wolves. He covered his mouth and poked his sister in the shoulder. Three extraordinarily large timber wolves were skulking about the edge of the forest, their elevated backs visible over the grass. The moose had not yet detected their presence.

The wolves made it about thirty feet away from the cow before it finally knew it had company. The moose bellowed loudly, so loudly that Claire dropped her final bit of canned ham, and turned towards the three over-sized creatures. It clearly had to decide whether to fight or flee.

It chose the latter, and as soon as it turned and bolted for the far side, the wolves did the same. The two largest wolves had caught up to the moose in seconds, a mere twenty feet from the safety of the trees.

One wolf bit a good chunk from the moose's back leg while the other took an even bigger chunk from its belly.

The moose stopped and made a run back towards where it came from, kicking its enormous hooves frantically, trying to trample the attacking pack.

The GEM LAKES

The wolves were relentless, and Claire was horrified at what came next. The moose was running in frantic circles, and soon Claire saw why. Four more wolves had appeared from all points around the clearing. They had the cow's only escape, the forest, successfully blocked off.

Claire could tell that the big animal was tiring, and it seemed to know that the wound in her belly would be fatal. She slowed as the first wolf took another vicious bite out of its hindquarters and it went halfway down. When she did that, the three attacking wolves pounced. The moose seemed to know that move and exploded from its prone position towards one of the guard wolves. The undersized wolf held its ground and snarled. The moose was delirious in pain and decided to take on one of its attackers head-on.

It never made it. The largest of the wolves literally leaped on to the cow's back and sank its powerful jaws into the moose's neck. It died before it landed on the ground.

Jake had not said a word during this entire scene, which he found both horrifying and fascinating.

Claire had already shrank away from the ridge, both hands covering her mouth in horror.

"Let's go quick," Jake whispered quickly. The wind was blowing off the meadow towards the lake. That was good. If it switched, and the wolves picked up their scent, they were in big trouble. The wolves were in a killing mood, and although he knew that the wolves would probably not be interested in humans, after what they had just witnessed, he was not going to take any chances.

He took one last look at the grisly scene below. All seven wolves were taking their share of the freshly killed meat. They were more than half done and would be finished soon.

Diamond Lake was a very beautiful lake, crystal clear with a white sandy bottom, as both Jake and Claire could tell from their view about fifty feet above the pristine waters. The trail from Sapphire ended abruptly, and if Jake had not caught the edge of the cliff in the corner of his eye, they would have plummeted to the bottom. They quickly consulted the map, which referred to this area as The Heights. Now he knew what it had meant. It was part of the trail to be sure, but the thin path ran out on the bare rock, with not much room for error. The wind from the lake smacked them directly in the face, which would make carrying the canoe overhead dangerous. One wrong gust and they would fall over the cliffs. It was a very long way down.

As it was, they had two choices. They could back-track quite a distance and join up with a path that seemed to lead *down* the cliff, although that seemed to be a treacherous and time consuming option. It was made that much more difficult by carrying a canoe. The second option was to simply jump. Claire made the decision for them, quickly and without need for consultation or consideration. "We aren't jumpin', so don't even think about it."

Jake was not really thinking about it, but nonetheless was annoyed by Claire's sudden dictatorship. "Did you even see another path back there? It's probably gone by now."

"We'll look for it then, and if we can't find it, maybe we should turn back!"

"We'll find it. Give me an hour."

"Fine, one hour, starting now."

They leaned down to pick up the canoe and caught a whiff of something very unpleasant. "What is that?" Claire gasped, pinching her nose.

Jake knew immediately that it was a skunk, but when he turned to face the odour head-on, he saw that it was actually six skunks. Large skunks. Jake shuddered.

A few summers ago, their old dog Lucky, in a decidedly unlucky sort of moment, came across a skunk behind Caribou Creek and took a direct shot of skunk stunk from a foot away. Their dad had filled the bathtub first with vinegar, then with tomato juice and had scrubbed him for three hours to get rid of the lingering smell.

The **GEM LAKES**

If you have never been sprayed by a skunk or have never been around something that has, you are (a) very fortunate and (b) unable to truly grasp the fear that the Lucknows now felt.

"Stay still," Claire whispered, "Maybe they'll go away."

The skunks seemed to hear Claire and hissed in defiance. They lurched towards them, stamping their feet. Their small heads and stubby legs looked ridiculous against their stout bodies and oversized bushy tails. The Lucknows automatically stepped back. They were running out of real estate in that particular direction, so Jake pulled the canoe carefully along with them.

"It'll be just like cliff jumping at the falls..."

"No way Jake!"

The skunks marched forwards. Their faces were divided in half by a thin white stripe that forked at the shoulders and then ran down each side of their glossy black fur, right to the tail—the very tail that they seemed ready and willing to spray with at any second.

"Don't look down, just stare at the other shore," he said soothingly, kicking the canoe over the edge.

"What are you doing?" she shrieked. That was enough to provoke the skunks, which had probably never laid eyes on such strange creatures in their lives. They spit and charged and Claire spun and took a flying jump off the edge of the cliff. Jake, somewhat shocked, quickly followed.

Claire's head was under water for only a few seconds, but when she popped her head above the surface, she bumped into the canoe, which had miraculously landed right side up.

Jake emerged another second later, grinning from ear to ear. "That was awesome!" he yelled.

They pulled the canoe to the nearest shore and took an inventory of themselves and their things. Besides being soaking wet, everything seemed in order, except their pack of food, which bounced right out the canoe on contact with the water.

"Great. What are we supposed to eat tonight?" Claire griped.

"We'll find something. Now let's go before it gets dark."

They had just pushed off the shore to cross the crystal lake, when Jake noticed a small geyser of water at his feet. The canoe had cracked when it hit the hard water—a twelve-inch split right on the seam of the floor.

"We've got a big problem up here!" he shouted.

He took off his ball cap and started bailing the water, while Claire continued paddling across the lake, hoping to make it across before the whole thing went down.

Jake managed to keep pace with the leak and Claire, who was becoming an expert paddler after these last few days, made good time across the calm water.

"Well, what are we going to do now?" Claire asked loudly. "We're only halfway there and we broke the canoe!"

"I hope you brought some chewing gum," he called back.

Ruby Lake is six hundred feet deep at its most shallow point. It drops straight from the shore like someone shot a hole right through the earth. In fact, that's very much what happened. Ruby Lake was created by a meteor strike ages ago, and is the deepest, and therefore coldest lake in the entire country. There was something very unsettling about being over a bottomless pit that could only be amplified by having a crack in your canoe, patched with only three sticks of peppermint gum and still sticky tree sap. Claire's stomach had butterflies as they stood and slipped the tip of the canoe into the chilly lake. She was not sure if they were butterflies or simply hunger pangs. What food they had left had been lost in the jump. They had not eaten since early that morning.

She found a stick from the forest and retrieved their dad's emergency lake kit from the tent bag. She took the fishing line out and tied it around the top of the stick. Dad had put a few Red Devils (these ones had hooks on them) in the kit, more than likely for Jake, and she took one of them and tied that to the other end.

"What are you doing?" Jake asked.

The GEM LAKES

"What does it look like?" she snapped. This whole thing was his idea and it seemed to be getting worse by the second. Not to mention the incredible amount of trouble that they were no doubt in already.

They carefully stepped into the canoe, even more carefully than usual, and gently pushed off the shore. It was more than odd not being able to see the bottom, even a foot away from the shore.

Halfway across Ruby's burgundy water, Claire flicked the red and white lure into the water. She was quite sure that her hunger pangs had devoured the butterflies in her stomach and she had now stooped to fishing as her only option for food. She hadn't seen a berry patch for hours, and she didn't hold much hope that she would see another one for a very long time. She didn't hold out much hope for fishing either. The one time that she had ever gone with Jake and her dad it had poured rain all morning. She had begged to go home but her father would have none of it. "This is when they bite hon! In the rain!" Needless to say, that had been her last time fishing.

Jake, at the front of the canoe, was dealing with two potential problems. One, the crack at his feet was seeping water steadily. He had to stop paddling every two minutes to bail the water with his baseball cap. He could just imagine it opening up, and him looking down into the black hole that was Ruby Lake.

Potential problem number two? What the heck were they going to do in the highly unlikely event that Claire actually caught a fish? She certainly wasn't going to touch it and he would bet the farm (if he owned one) that she expected him to deal with it. That would be an ugly scene.

It did not take until the end of that very thought for one of the two issues to become a reality.

"Jake, I think I've got one!"

At the mere idea of having to unhook the fish himself, Jake broke out in a sweat. *Please don't get it in the canoe, please don't, please.* Even worse, with Claire's stick obviously having no tension control whatsoever, and her hunger encouraging a death grip on the "rod," the fish pulled Claire into the water instead. New problem...bigger problem!

Claire fell sideways into the lake, and as Jake tried to shift his weight to balance the wobbled canoe, he only ended up flinging himself out the other side, flipping the canoe completely upside down. The lifejackets, which had been used instead as cushions for the canoe seats since Opal Lake, were trapped underneath the overturned boat. Lifejackets, of course, lose their effectiveness when not actually being worn.

The frigid water shocked Jake, but when he popped up, he could only think of Claire, whom he could not see, and he swam frantically to where she went under. He was surprised when her head appeared right in front of him.

"Something's got me!" she screamed. The fishing stick had either been ripped from her hands or she had simply let go when she had hit the water. Nonetheless, something had a firm grip on her foot and was pulling her under the surface. Jake grabbed her under her arms and tried to pull her towards the crippled canoe.

Something was pulling her! Jake and Claire both started flailing madly, smack in the middle of the deepest lake in Canada, with God-knows-what trying to drag them to their watery grave. The desperate kicking got them beside the canoe without them even realizing it. Jake tried to flip the canoe and did, but it was now half filled with water.

"Grab the side and kick!" Jake shouted.

"I am kicking! It's still got me!" Jake had never seen his sister's eyes that wide. They only grew wider at the sight of their swamped canoe slowly disappearing below the surface of the water. Claire's head had started to dip under the water too. She tried to scream but received only a mouthful of water. He was so scared for her that what happened next can only be attributed to pure adrenaline.

Jake grabbed her again under her arms and flipped onto his back, cradling her on his chest. Despite the numbing water, or maybe because of it, Jake swam steadily and quickly towards the far shore. He did not think about the sickening depth of the water. He put out of his mind the creature that had his sister's leg, and he shook off the fact that he had not swam any real distance in two or three years.

About halfway there, something wrapped around his body from behind. At first, Jake thought it was another creature from the deep, like the one that still had Claire's leg. Its coloured appendages almost covered his head and he screamed in horror. It was the tent.

He grabbed it instinctively and tucked it under his arm. Now he was dragging Claire, whatever was pulling Claire, and the tent.

The distance was only half a mile, but seemed like a hundred by the time Jake's frozen hands reached the opposite shore. He clawed his way onto the red mud and pulled Claire in a few moments later.

She was sobbing now, great heaves of resignation. She was convinced she was going to die. As Jake pulled her onto the safety of the ground, he steeled himself and looked at her leg, which he half expected to be gnawed right off. There, on the end of her shoe, was the fishing line, hopelessly tangled around her sneaker. At the end of the line, thrashing like, well, like a fish out of water, was the biggest pickerel that Jake had ever seen. It had snapped the tip off Claire's stick and would have escaped cleanly if not for catching around the tip of Claire's foot.

Claire kicked off her shoe as a reflex action, relieved that she still appeared intact. Jake, whose muscles and lungs were aching desperately for oxygen, stared at the giant fish. It was as thick as a football. Streaks of black, yellow and green coloured its back and side. Jake looked at it dumbly, waiting for the prickly dorsal fin to go down. In between flips and flops, it finally did, and Jake, taking a deep breath, grabbed the fish behind its head. He almost lost his grip right away, drastically underestimating the weight. He grabbed the slippery tail with his other hand, and there it was.

It seemed like a very small moment in time, especially after his sprint swim, but to Jake, it was the proudest moment of his life. He was holding the fish. He moved his hand from the top of the fish to the bottom, behind the gills, like his dad always did when he posed for pictures. Jake stared at the massive wall eyes of the pickerel and laughed. The laughter consumed the last bit of energy that Jake's body had to offer. The adrenaline was crashing down and so was Jake. He passed out in the soft red sand.

It took only seconds for Claire to wake her brother up. She was screaming and yelling at the fish as it thrashed and flipped on the ground, dangerously close to making its way back to the water's edge. Dinner was making a hasty escape.

Jake was too slow to react so Claire ran to the sandy edge and grabbed what was left of the fishing line. The Red Devil had hooked the mighty fish clean through the top lip and Claire pulled it away from the edge, the fine fishing line cutting into the flesh of her hands.

She let go of the line as the fish reached her feet. Her dad had never brought anything *that* big back from *his* fishing trips! Jake was suddenly beside her, a short club-like stick in his right hand.

"What are you going to do?" she asked.

"We have to kill it."

"What?"

"Well, if you want to *eat* it, it would be better if it were dead."

"Right...right."

"Don't worry, it won't feel anything."

Jake had watched his dad do this countless times but had never tried it himself. "We have to bop it on the head. It's got a soft spot on the top."

The pickerel, none too pleased about being abducted from the lake, started flopping in that direction again. It definitely had a nose for the water.

The stick came down swift and hard. The fish stopped moving.

"Is it dead?" Claire wondered. Her eyes were now wider than the pickerel's.

"I think so."

Jake and Claire got on their knees and inspected the fish, their noses just inches away. They looked for signs of breathing but saw none. "Do fish have a pulse?" Jake asked aloud, gently touching it around the gills.

"I think it's dead," he finally declared.

Claire nodded in agreement. Their dinner was dead. Now what?

"Is there a knife in dad's survival kit?" Jake asked her.

"Yes."

"Where is it?"

She looked out onto the water. "If it's not at the bottom of the lake, it will be soon."

"Great, that's just great. We're going to need something sharp. Start looking for a broken rock or something."

They scanned the ground for ten minutes and then met back at the fish, which by then had drawn the attention of more than a few flies.

"Nothing?"

"Nothing."

Jake was about to give up. The meat would spoil if they didn't clean it soon. Then, out of the blue, there was the answer...right on top of his sister's head.

"Why are you staring at me?"

"What's keeping your hair pulled back?" he inquired rhetorically.

"Bobbie pins. Why?"

"Give me one."

She was too tired and too hungry to put up an argument. She pulled a pin out and handed it over. Jake took it and knelt down on the gravelly ground. He picked up a small rock and started grinding the tip of the pin against it. In moments, the dull pin had become a sharp point.

"We need to make a fire."

"I guess you'll be happy that I kept the water-proof matches in my pocket instead of the kit," she said as she produced the pack with a dramatic flourish.

Jake had always thought that Lucknow had seemed miscast as a name for his family. How about Luck-when? First it was Grandpa, then he with his tumour. Where was the luck in that? Bad luck maybe. They go on a canoe trip and they sink the freakin' canoe. The pots, gone. The food, gone. Sunscreen, bug spray, clothing—gone, gone, gone. It was more accurately Luck-none.

On the bright side, the fire had started on the second try. The sopping tent was stretched out to dry beside it. As Jake was hanging their only shelter, he noticed a heavy lump in the bottom of the tent. His heart raced as he hoped it was another fish, caught in the tent like a net. Instead, he pulled out a very wet red and white sweater. Jake groaned loudly. "Merry freakin' Christmas."

The fish had a stick through its mouth all the way through its body and out under the tail. The stick was set up like a barbecue spit, with two forked branches on either side of the fire supporting the weight of their dinner.

Jake had used the sharpened bobbie pin to split open the pickerel's belly. He had pulled the guts out and simply stuck the stick through it. It wasn't the way his dad would have done it but a hair pin had a way of severely limiting the options.

The flames licked at the underside of the fish, the scales crisping and peeling off. Jake's and Claire's stomachs ached from the familiar smell.

After turning the fish over a few times, Jake declared it done and they tore into the tender meat like wild dogs. The soft bones pulled away from the meat easily and before they knew it, they were done.

"I don't think I've ever eaten that much fish in my life!" Claire exclaimed.

"Neither have I. I could probably have some more though." Jakes appetite was returning with a vengeance. He was not sure why. Sometimes, back at the cabin, the mere act of eating caused him to be sick. He guessed that it was because he had stopped taking the pills.

"Not me. I'm stuffed." Claire felt the tent. It was still damp. She didn't care.

"Let's put this up, I'm not sleeping out here."

Jake was so tired he thought that if he just closed his eyes, he could probably sleep anywhere. Reluctantly, he pushed himself up to help Claire pitch the tent.

They awoke in the tent early the next morning, the air inside as hot as a sauna and smelling strongly of mildew. It was six-thirty in the morning, a time of day that Claire had only heard about before, when they could no longer stand the suffocating air and evacuated. Claire, while washing her face at the lakeshore, made a startling discovery—both the flashlights had drifted to shore and were bobbing within arm's reach of the red mud. It was just like her dad to buy floating flashlights! She left her own light by the water's edge, as it was useless and just one more thing to carry. Jake's flashlight, however, worked fine.

"It looks like a hot one," Jake said. "We're going to have to get a long way before the afternoon."

They would be on foot the rest of the way, but neither of them uttered a word about how they would be getting back with no canoe. They were both thinking the same thing, which was Grandpa *had* to be alive, if for no other reason than to get them back home safely.

By nine-thirty, three hours later, the heat intensified to the point that it was hard to breathe. It was so muggy that their clothes clung to them like a second skin. It reminded Claire of wearing a damp wet suit.

Rob Keough

They plodded down a path of brown pine needles where gnarled tree roots stuck out from the trail like starched bony fingers reaching up through the ground, trying to pull them under. They kept tripping and stubbing their toes, each time adding just an ounce more frustration to the situation. Neither one spoke for the mere act of breathing seemed more like sucking steam. Sweat ran into their eyes even when they stood completely still. Claire could not recall feeling more disgusting and uncomfortable. Not even noon, the worst was yet to come. They would have to find shelter from the sweltering sun.

Bob Lucknow stood on his dock and watched the sky. The air was dead calm a moment ago, but now the birch tree's leaves started to flicker in a slight breeze. As often happens after a terribly hot and humid day, a summer storm was brewing...and it was going to be a good one. The thunderheads in the distance were turning from blue-gray to ugly black. A group of loons sitting in the middle of the lake started calling, usually the most haunting, beautiful sound heard in nature. These loons, however, kept calling louder and louder, so nervous that it sounded like a crazy laugh. Uneasiness crept under Bob's skin.

He paced back and forth on the dock. The old wooden boards creaked under his weight. He had designed and built the dock himself, which explained the heavy lean to the left. After a few glasses of wine, that lean seemed to become a serious angle, an angle he had overcompensated for on one occasion two summers ago, much to the humour and delight of his children.

He was worried about them. What parent wouldn't be? But his was a different worry than his wife's. He may not know where they were, but he was quite sure where they were headed. He glanced over to his right, where the dense trees cloaked the Mad Trapper's cabin. If the kids were going where he thought they were, it could have only been the trapper that pointed them in that direction. One of the kids must have stumbled into him in the woods just as he himself had twenty years ago. He would pay a visit to the old trapper later. Right now, however, he turned his attention back to the sky.

A wall of black cloud had swallowed the sun whole an hour ago and now towered above them like it would consume the entire earth.

The sheer vastness of the billowing clouds choked out the light completely, but not before Jake stopped in his tracks, resulting in Claire almost bumping him over.

"What is it? What do you see?" Claire was on edge. She could feel the awful change in the atmosphere—that high-charged, hair-on-the-back-of-your neck feeling that came right before a good storm. Claire had never understood why her father always said, "Here comes a good storm!" Thunder terrified her and by association, so did lightning.

Jake held up a hand and pointed through the trees ahead of them with the other.

Both siblings cringed. The shadowy figures that watched them on Emerald were back, although Jake did not think that they had seen them yet. He kept perfectly still.

The mumblers were moving quickly through the forest from all sides, but weren't concerned in the least about them. They were all rushing towards a towering hump of rock that seemed out of place in the middle of nowhere. It was a mine.

They were taking cover from the mother of all storms that was forming above them. Maybe the mumblers were scared of thunder too.

"Let's get out of here. This way," Jake motioned to Claire. If those creatures were looking for shelter, then they had better follow suit. They sure weren't going to share accommodations with those lunatics. As they ran away from the mine, Jake wondered for a moment what they could possibly have been digging for out here.

Rob Keough

The Succa Sunna Mining Company drilled their first test hole in 1921 and the two French-Canadian cousins who co-owned the fledging company must have thought that they hit the iron ore lottery. Within eleven months, the mine was operating with a crew of ninety men, and ten months after that it was the most productive iron mine in North America.

Ruby Lake, located only half a mile from the mine's slag pile, took its name from the iron rich, red dirt that surrounded it. The mine grew so productive that a national railway company started the process of surveying and extending a track right past the mine to shorten the distance that the company trucks had to travel on the deeply rutted dirt roads.

But in 1924, March 30th to be exact, that all changed the day the earth's magnetic axis flipped. For most of the men, both the miners and the rail workers, the change was gradual; fatigue, insomnia, sore joints, then raging fevers that would break as fast as they came on. Then the accidents started. Two railroaders were killed when a load of ties broke loose from their steel binding, three more when the dynamite charges they were preparing exploded prematurely.

The miners were faring no better. Three sudden cave-ins killed twenty-six workers. Two explosions deep in the mine killed ten more, including one of the founding cousins.

There were disappearances too. Seven miners and thirteen rail workers vanished in their sleep or while alone in the woods, a trail of blood the only trace of them.

When the Great Depression hit in 1929, it gave the railway the perfect excuse to pull the line. That, combined with the plunging world markets, was the end of the Succa Sunna Mining Company. A skeleton crew was left behind to clean up and seal the mine entrance.

Many years later, when the economy had pulled itself out of the ruins, cabins started popping up on the shorelines of what is now Lampshine Lake, which sat right beside the railway's sparkling new main line, fifty kilometres to the south of the abandoned track on Ruby Lake. With new summer cottages being built, so too were power lines to provide electricity. The hydro crews managed to place only eleven poles when four workers were killed in five days. An animal that nobody had managed to even lay eyes on had attacked them and dragged them into the forest where they were never found. The hydro company immediately declared the rock "unsuitably hard" for their poles, a flimsy way of saying, "We've read the history books. We're out of here!"

The lake was nicknamed 'Lampshine' because the only way to get light or heat was from an oil lamp and later propane. Even today, on the north shore of Opal Lake, those eleven poles still stand awkwardly out of a naked base of granite rock. All eleven have been scorched by lightning strikes over the years, an ominous reminder to future hydro crews.

And Hydro has taken notice. Even now, if you were so inclined to phone them to inquire about running power lines to Lampshine Lake, they would politely dismiss you, telling you the consumer versus amp usage ratio was too low to consider lines. Just an updated version of "the rock is unsuitably hard." There would never, ever, be power at Lampshine Lake.

The thunder had started rumbling from far away, then seemed to roll towards Jake and Claire like freight trains on a collision course. The first thunderclap shook the ground, no rumbling, no rolling, just a sonic boom that hurt their ears.

The rain came in unrelenting sheets—torrents of icy water unleashed by the angry clouds all at once. The wind blew hard from the north but swirled violently as it neared the ground, making it seem like it was coming from every direction. In seconds, for the third time in twenty-four hours, they were completely drenched.

Lightning bolts sizzled from the black sky, so close that the deafening thunderclap was almost simultaneous. Jake could see that Claire was screaming but the terrible wind was carrying her shrieks away with the cutting rain.

He grabbed her arm and started running straight ahead, into the forest and away from the open path. The trees offered some protection from wind, but Jake was worried about lightning hitting the tall tops. They kept running, through pools of rainwater that suddenly formed rushing creeks. The forest's drainage system was hard at work and presently overloaded.

The stone igloo came out of nowhere, just sitting there in the woods on the hump of rock that spread over the forest floor. Jake had no idea what the purpose of the igloo was, or even if an animal or a human had built it, but it showed no signs that it had been occupied anytime recently. It seemed solid enough for the purpose that Jake needed—shelter.

He pulled Claire to the ground and they crawled through the opening of the hut, hoping that some animal had not had the same idea. Inside, it was pitch dark and Jake wiped the water from his eyes and tried to adjust his vision. He could hear teeth chattering and it was a moment before he realized they were his. He felt around for the pack of waterproof matches, hoping that they were a whole lot drier than he was. His soaked shirt clung to his cold skin and it was not hard to locate the waterlogged box. The box itself was mostly mush, but the green-tipped matchsticks seemed only damp. There were three left.

"Hurry, I'm so cold."

Lightning flashed through every open space between the rocks, and the thunderclap that followed shook the whole shelter. Jake did not understand how the roof did not cave in on them. The rain, for the most part, stayed outside, unable to penetrate the stone structure. Some water dripped from the top but neither Lucknow noticed...they could not get any wetter.

The first match snapped in half, and when Jake tried to salvage it, the wax coating ripped off, rendering it useless. Suddenly, the pressure was on. He could not afford to break the last two matches. He held the second match gently between his fingers and struck it against the sandpaper side of the box. It sparked once and then roared to life. Jake and Claire used the dim light to look around the hut. They immediately saw what the igloo had been used for. All around them were what looked at first to be large firecrackers. They were actually bundled sticks of dynamite—sticks and sticks of dynamite.

"Put it out! Put it out!"

The wind howled, reminding them that they couldn't leave. Claire started crying and Jake put his arms around her, shivering to the bone.

The next morning they awoke to a sopping forest. As they crawled out of the stale air of the dynamite filled hut, they found themselves in the middle of a ghost town in the dull, cool morning.

Beads of water clung to every blade of grass. Everything they had, including themselves, was damp. A stiff breeze shook water off of the leaves of trees and showered the kids all over again.

Claire was shivering from the cold that had set in her bones; her flesh was bumpy with what she thought might be a permanent case of goosebumps.

It didn't really look like there was even a cloud in the sky, but more like someone had become tired of amethyst blue and had taken a paint roller across it in a very leaden gray.

Claire hated these days, as it always brought her mood down two or three notches. At the rate things were going, she didn't know if she could afford those notches today. Not to mention, she definitely needed the sun to poke through and thaw her out.

There were actually three of the stone igloos, one of which had collapsed into a pile of rocks. There were broken down carts and wheelbarrows that held no rainwater because of so many holes. Their wooden spokes and axles were either petrified or rotting, the metal covering bubbling brown with rust. A few metres into the trees, a row of crumbling cabins was sinking into the ground, each one with an ancient woodstove and the skeletons of metal bedframes.

Some of them still had the thin, shredded mattress fused on them by time, torn apart by birds and mice. Hundreds, maybe thousands of tin cans were piled behind the cabins, creating a metal mountain in the middle of nowhere. Behind the cabins was the outline of the mine itself, something that both Lucknows wanted to avoid more than anything.

As they turned to head away from Ruby Lake, they passed a scattered pile of sun-bleached bones. It sent chills down their spines until they realized that they didn't belong to human beings. They were horse bones, or maybe oxen that had pulled the never-ending loads of rocks from the mine to the slag piles. By the number of bones, it didn't look like they got more than a few weeks out of each animal. They shifted their direction again, anxious to get the Succa Sunna Mining Company behind them.

Bob Lucknow was holding something back. He was keeping something from his wife and Major Shocklot as well, although he has a sneaking suspicion that the Major was holding back from him too. There could be no other explanation as to why the search for his children had stalled. Shocklot knew exactly what was in those lakes. Bob felt like a poker player with a million-dollar pot, and both men were bluffing each other with generous amounts of bull.

This is why Bob Lucknow was now sitting across from the Mad Trapper in the old man's isolated cabin, on the very same wolfskin-covered couch that Jake had a few days ago. He needed to know if the Major was playing with the same deck he was.

"You couldn't leave well enough alone could you?"

The Mad Trapper grinned innocently, his leathery face rumpling into hundreds of little valleys. "Now, now Bobby, I just told him the truth, didn't I? I didn't paddle him across to Opal. He did that himself."

"Did you give him the map?"

The trapper nodded. "I could see in his eyes that he was goin' anyway. He might as well go the right way I reckon."

"You reckoned, did you?"

"I did."

"Well that's fantastic. Did you even remember what it's like back there? You "reckoned" that they could find their way safely?"

"That boy of yours is full of other things besides that tumour Bobby. Piss and vinegar come to mind. The boys got a stubborn streak wider than your old man's."

"What about his sister?"

"He'll get them out safely. No harm will come."

"What if Dad's not alive anymore?"

The trapper seemed to consider this. "We'll give it a few days, see what comes of it."

"These aren't beavers in your trapline! They're my kids!"

The Mad Trapper's eyes grew dark. "It's been more that a few years since you've been back ain't it? It's more dangerous for you now than then. You're more than a few steps slower these days. Why do you think those boys with the toys won't go in there?"

Jake tripped over the steel rail of the train track or he may have never even noticed it was there. Weeds and wild grass had sprouted between the limestone ballast, covering the uncompleted track, which had formed golden rust after decades of no use. This was the track that would have led past the mine.

The stones were rough walking, and the kids jumped down from the abandoned rail. They came across a stack of creosote-stained ties that were left by the track, waiting and waiting to be put to good use.

"Remember when we used to put coins on the track?" Claire asked. Five or six years ago, while waiting for the chronically late train to take them back to the city one Sunday, Jake and Claire had badgered their dad into giving them some coins, so the passing freight trains would flatten them into thin medallions.

Bob had been half-asleep at the time and he grunted that he had some coins in his jacket pocket, which was doubling at that particular moment as a pillow.

Find them they did, and they carefully laid the coins out on the smooth steel rail and marked it with a rock so they could keep a reference point when the speeding train would flip them off. It was only twenty minutes before the first freight went by, blasting its horn and rumbling past. They recovered all but one of the twelve coins.

Afterwards, heading home on the passenger train, they showed off their freshly minted treasures.

"My Lord—those are the flattest pennies I've ever seen!" Bob looked closer. They seemed more silver than copper. "These are pennies right?" he asked suspiciously. The kids nodded their heads in anxious unison. Susan started snickering. There was definitely a blotch of gold in the middle of all eleven pieces.

"Quarters?" Even then he started checking his jacket pockets. He turned them inside out. Empty.

"Toonies! You used my toonies?"

The kids did not understand the problem. They had asked after all. "We asked you."

Bob sputtered, "That's over twenty bucks!" Still, the kids did not get his point. "Twenty bucks..." his voice trailed off. Susan had doubled over laughing. He had turned to his wife, "When we were kids we used pennies. Didn't we use pennies?" He had turned to his children; "From now on *you two* will use pennies!" They thought they were in trouble but then their dad started laughing too.

Claire looked back at the old track. She missed the train. "It's been a while since we flattened coins."

Duncan Shocklot was barely able to crush out his cigarette in time. It was a filthy habit he had kicked ten years ago, but in stressful moments such as this, he snuck the occasional puff. He never smoked in front of his men and had thought that walking ten minutes behind the Lucknow outhouse had been far enough...until Bob Lucknow himself broke through the bushes beside him.

"Out for a walk Mr. Lucknow?" he coughed.

Bob looked surprised for only a moment. "Yeah, just trying to clear my head," he smiled and began to walk away.

"Conscience giving you trouble Mr. Lucknow?"

Bob stopped dead in his tracks. "What do you mean by that?"

"Nothing. Nothing at all. It just seems to me that if it were my kids back there...well, I might be reacting a little more like your wife is. I just get the feeling that you might know more than you're letting on...that's all." He looked over Bob's shoulder, into the forest where he had just come from. "Seems like a lot of trails around here are more cleared out than that one."

"Just a change of pace."

"Uh huh. Look Mr. Lucknow, let me be frank with you. We know all about your father's disappearance and all about Mr. Worrell over there."

Worrell. That was a name he had not heard in a very long time. "We know he didn't kill your father. I just need to find out if he knows anything about your kids."

Bob's shoulders slumped. "Jake ran into him the other day in the forest. He gave him a map through the Gem Lakes."

"A map? Of the Gem Lakes? Have you seen this map?"

"Yes. My father and Worrell made it many, many years ago."

"I think it's time we had a chat with this 'Mad Trapper'."

The cabin looked the same from the outside as it had twenty minutes earlier, except for one thing—the Mad Trapper was gone. As they entered the cabin, Bob noticed a fine layer of dust had settled over everything in the place. The air felt cold, even though it was twenty-five degrees outside.

"And you say you were here an hour ago?"

"Less than that," Bob replied honestly. "He'll probably be back soon."

The Major sniffed. "He's gone. He's a trapper, which means he's a tracker. He's the kind of person the military hires to teach us these things. We'd have a better chance of finding a ghost than him."

Bob thought he was joking at first. By the tone of his voice, it was apparent that he was not.

PART THREE

A majestic bald eagle, wearing a great hood of white and soaring along effortlessly with the air currents, had a perfectly clear view of the goings on of the Lucknow children, who seemed to be heading where no person their age should be heading. Perhaps as a warning, it let out a squawk.

Jake was watching the eagle as well. It glided in a circle above them, watching. He turned his eyes to the ground when it seemed to squawk at him. On Lampshine, Jake and his father used to watch a pair of eagles feed on the fish remains after they had dumped them on Fish Gut Island, across the bay from their cabin. The "island" was really only the tip of a rock that peaked above the surface of the water. All the cottagers dumped their fish remains there so the stink wouldn't attract bears to the cabins. Fish Gut Island constantly gleamed with fish scales and was stained with blood. It was like a take-out restaurant for birds.

The eagles just sat there, perched high in the trees waiting...waiting for some fisherman to discard his waste. They were drawn to the drone of the boat motors, like a dinner bell signalling that the food was ready. The seagulls would get whatever scraps the eagles left.

This eagle was bigger, and Jake was uneasy about the squawk. He often thought that the eagles from Lampshine could pick him up and take him away if they had been so inclined. This one could probably take both of them at the same time.

It didn't seem too interested in feeding though, it just watched, in big, looping circles.

The rock that they were walking on, right on the edge of the lake, sloped gently into a valley of pine trees before sloping back up again on the far side. The basin was crowded with pines, each one seemingly fighting for its own bit of space. The soothing smell of pure pine wafted up on the rock from the gentle breeze off the water. They would have to make their way through the valley to get to the other side. Dusk was knocking on the door, like a gentle reminder that neither Lucknow needed. Night, once again, was on its way.

They descended the bare rock carefully and made their way into the trees. What light was left in the day could not penetrate the thick coverage of the tree branches. The needles on the trees looked soft and gentle but were in fact sharp and pointed, and if the angle was just right (or wrong as Jake looked at it) it felt very much like the sting of a wasp.

Spiderwebs, as soft as silk, were spun from seemingly every branch. They were not like the decrepit, yellowed cobwebs that were on the porch of the cabin. They had a strange, intricate beauty about them—at least to Jake.

When they emerged from the other side, they were completely covered in sticky pine needles and spiderwebs that clung like fine hairs.

They reached the opposite side of Moonstone Lake just before dark. Having to walk *around* the lake instead of canoeing across it added two or three hours to their trip.

It would soon become very apparent where the lake took its name. As Claire tried to untie a knot to get the still damp tent bag open, a cloud moved listlessly across the night sky. In itself, it was no cause for alarm, for it was not a thunderhead or even a simple rain cloud. What it had been doing, up till now, was covering the luminous white moon. The shrill howling began almost immediately after the last tail of cloud exposed the lunar light—wolves.

Jake froze. Claire did the same. The howling was so close that it seemed to encircle them. They had never heard a more unforgettable and piercing sound.

"Keep the tent in the bag!" Jake hissed. They could not stay here. The memory of that pack taking down the moose was still vivid in their minds. They had been savage and quick. They had been coldly methodical. He did not like his chances hanging on the thickness of one layer of nylon. He was not sure he wouldn't have felt the same with two inches of steel.

"Let's run for the last lake. Can you do it?"

Claire nodded furiously. Anywhere he was going, she would be right behind.

Jake took the tent from her and tucked it under his arm like a football. They found the path with the flashlight and then ran, following the bobbing light.

Soon the light beam from the flashlight was being caught in other beams of light that Jake at first thought were other flashlights from other people. It was the moonstones, rocks that caught the reflection of the moon and beamed them off other stones, like a rock star light show. It was this that was making the wolves howl even louder until they sounded like they were right on top of them. It turns out they were.

A golden wolf, as tall as Claire, stepped in front of their path. With each turn of the flashlight, the beam found only the shining blue eyes of another member of the pack. There was very suddenly nowhere to hide—no trees to climb, no rocks to hide behind, no river to jump into. They were completely surrounded. And then, suddenly, silence. From the maddening howling to utter stillness, the wolves' attention was redirected away from the moon.

Jake had seen a wolf this close only once before, on the gravel road into Lampshine. It had looked like a big dog. Like everything else Jake had seen in the Gem Lakes, these were different.

They were thicker, longer; their snouts seemed bigger and their tongues lapped over their oversized fangs in a hideous manner. This was clearly the same pack they had seen in the meadow. Thankfully, they had cleaned the blood of the moose from their muzzles.

The GEM LAKES

They did not make a move. They just stared at the children. It was in this exact moment that Jake realized that he was tired of waiting for others to make the first move. He was tired of a lot of things; he was tired of being tired, he was tired of being sick and most of all, he was tired of being scared.

Jake grabbed Claire's hand. This was going to be their rite of passage, just like that television show Jake had seen with the Africans walking over the red-hot coals. These wolves were his red-hot coals. He squeezed her hand. "Let's go."

On cue, the wolves howled.

Claire closed her eyes, Jake kept his open, watching the wolf that was in their path walk slowly backwards and then turn, as if it wanted to be followed.

The flashlight had changed from a white light to yellow, the batteries slowly dying; no doubt their life had been leeched from their time in the water. The moonstones, however, continued to throb and bounce moon beams off each other. The lead wolf seemed to be shaking with excitement, like it had better things to do than lead them to the Lake of the Clouds.

The rest of the pack followed behind. Neither Jake nor Claire could be sure of their exact numbers as they kept slipping in and out of the brilliant light beams. Occasionally, they would sense wolves only a few feet behind them, and other times they would catch glimpses of shadowy figures weaving through the dark forest beside them.

They walked all night, hours and hours through the chilly air, never taking their eyes off the tawny leader. Tiredness never came to them but that was easily explained considering the supersized pack of wild dogs surrounding them.

It was an hour past sunrise when Claire turned around and saw that the pack was no longer tailing them. When she looked in front of them a few seconds later, she saw that their guide had disappeared as well.

"Where'd he go?"

Jake had taken his eyes off of him for only a second and did not see where he went. One thing for certain, it certainly didn't make any noise when it went.

The forest opened suddenly into a rock flat that overlooked a small pond. They had passed several of these openings over the course of the trip. This one seemed no different, except for the tall pile of neatly stacked wood that was set in between two tree trunks. They stood in front of the woodpile—neither daring to say what first came to their mind.

A very thick tree had been uprooted from its rocky base and blown over, perhaps in the windstorm. Jake and Claire walked by it without much thought and almost fell straight into a concaved rock. It was more than that. It was somebody's fire pit. A single log still glowed under a thin blanket of white ash. A blackened coffeepot and a heat-deformed pan sat on top of a flat rock that had been set beside the pit like a stovetop.

"Jake..."

Jake nodded. They were close to somebody. They were close to Grandpa.

"Jake!"

"I see it already. Look around for a..." he halted in mid-sentence, finally catching a glimpse of what Claire was already staring at. The overturned tree had most definitely not come down in last night's wind. There were no roots to be seen at the base of the monstrous tree, just a wall made of rocks and old boards...and a small wooden door, large enough to crawl through. It was somebody's home. They had stumbled into somebody's front yard!

"Do you think it's him?" Claire asked. Jake did not want to consider the options. Maybe it wasn't him at all, but some other trapper, maybe madder than the Mad Trapper. Maybe it was one of the fast talkers from the mine. Maybe it was Grandpa, but maybe he was sick or even dead. He didn't come all this way to discover his body.

He reached for the door.

"Shouldn't we at least knock?" Claire asked, grabbing her brother's arm.

She was right, of course; even in the middle of nowhere, it was still good form to be polite. Jake rapped on the door three times.

There was no sound at all. Nobody rustling to get clothes on, nobody yelling, "*Who is it?*" Just an eerie silence.

Jake grabbed the wooden pull handle and gave it a good yank. The door was stiff but popped open easily enough, and the Lucknows found themselves face-to-face with a double-barreled shotgun.

A wiry old man was crouched in the hut, his slate black eyes contrasting against his long white hair. He held the shotgun steady and pushed his way outside the hut. Stepping onto even ground, he straightened until he towered over them. He had a fantastic handlebar moustache, as white as a snow goose but unruly without the sculpting effects of a good wax. His eyes, which had appeared black in the shadows of the hut, were actually a deep blue that sparkled in the light of the sun.

"Who the blazes are you two?" he rasped.

Their voices were caught in their throats, afraid that any sound at all might trigger the gun to go off.

"You all deaf or something? How did you get here?" His voice was rising, prompting Jake and Claire to burst forth every answer to every question that the gun-wielder could possibly ask. He stepped back and held up a heavily callused hand. It was then that they saw the crazy man couldn't have pulled the trigger anyway. He was missing his right hand all together! "Whoa, Whoa, Whoa there." He lowered his gun, "How...did...you...get... here?"

Jake felt instant relief from the lowered weapon. "We canoed...walked the last bit I guess."

"From?"

"Lampshine Lake sir."

The bushman grunted. "Lampshine? What's your name boy?"

"Jake. Jake Lucknow."

The bushman did not throw down the gun and embrace either of them, nor did his thin lips crack a smile. His eyes flashed only a little. If this was his Grandpa, Jake had been expecting a little happier reaction.

"We're looking for Gordon Lucknow. Do you know where he is?"

He raised a bushy eyebrow, "What would you two want from old Gordo?"

Jake's heart skipped a beat. "He's our Grandpa." The second brow arched, "Your Grandpa, eh?" He put his chin down and turned around. Jake thought he noticed a look of sadness pass over his face before he put his back to them. "You came a mite too late, I'm afraid. Follow me."

A few minutes later the children were standing over a recently-dug grave. A steel re-bar tied in the shape of a cross marked the spot. "I got the metal from the old track. The railroad buried their own like this…it was easier than carrying them out."

Claire covered her eyes; Jake could not tear his away from the grave. He bit he lower lip so hard that it bled. This could not be right. "But when…"

The bushman actually looked pained. "You just missed him. Faded fast 'bout ten day ago. He passed on yesterday morn'."

Yesterday morning. They had missed him by one day. Jake would have nothing to leave his family. One day…The bushman stepped back and left them alone with their crushing disappointment.

Jake and Claire found the old man back in the mud hut, rummaging through a small pack for something that was apparently eluding him.

"I'm making some tea if you'd like some," he offered. He probably felt bad for them, Jake supposed. Nonetheless, he shook his head.

"I'll have some please," Claire said. She was so thirsty that she would have drunk tomato juice at this point.

The back of their necks blared fire-engine red, the direct result of their tube of sunscreen sinking to the dark depths of Ruby Lake. This prompted the old man to declare them "a couple of lobsters fresh from the cookin' pot."

"You're surely going to regret that in the morning," he added.

Claire was beginning to regret it already. A pulsating ache was developing right behind her eyes.

The GEM LAKES

"Sun sickness," the bushman said, "You're lucky you had caps on or I'd have found you dried up like raisins somewhere."

Jake examined the inside of the hut more closely. There were wooden planks laid on the floor, but they were loose and dirt came up through the cracks when they were stepped on. The bushman had built some shelves out of tree branches that held very old looking books. On the floor were a sleeping bag and a pile of wool blankets, apparently the man's bed.

The bushman noticed Jake examining his home. "Built like a castle," he said proudly, "Pine branches, mud, more pine branches, rocks, and more mud. A herd of caribou could have a barnyard dance on that roof and wouldn't do no harm."

"Do you live here in the winter?" Jake asked. Despite the anguish of his failed mission, he was fascinated that somebody could live like this.

"What? You think I sleep in a snow bank? A candle will keep this place warm in the coldest winter frost."

"Did Grandpa live with you?"

The bushman scoffed. "Are you kidding? I liked Gordo and all, but this place isn't big enough for two grown men. Your granddad had a little place on the Lake of the Clouds."

"I'd like to see it. Will you take us there?"

The bushman hesitated slightly, "I guess we can swing by there later. I've got a canoe stashed on the south shore."

Claire was still looking at the gun, which the old man had only just leaned against the dirt wall. "What do you have that for?"

"I got my reasons…it doesn't work no more anyway. Don't reckon I even have shells for it."

"Then why do you keep it?"

"It puts on a good show don't it? Some animals around here remember when it did work and they got themselves a hide full of lead. Most of 'em turn tail and run at just the look of it…most of 'em."

Jake and Claire set about making themselves useful in the eyes of the bushman. The strategy now was to get on and stay on this strange man's good side.

Dusk settled in slowly, and the Lucknow children made their way to the woodpile to gather firewood for the night. Less than halfway there, the bugs had beaten them back to the camp and continued their persistent assault for the next half hour.

The bushman seemed unfazed and grumbled something unintelligible on his way past the kids, who were flapping their arms in desperation.

The old man returned, carrying a stack of wood so high that you could not see his head. When he dropped the wood by the fire pit, it revealed that the old man was wearing some sort of new hat. Upon closer inspection, it was simply a branch off a pine tree. He had strapped it to his head with what appeared to be fishing line. He looked utterly ridiculous.

The kids looked at each other with some concern. They weren't sure if he was trying to be funny or if he had lost his marbles. It seemed he couldn't afford to lose many more.

The branch dropped down in front of his eyes and past the back of his neck so he looked like a pine tree with lips.

"Bug protection," he stated.

"It looks weird," Claire replied. Jake nodded his agreement.

"Me? Take a look at each other!"

They did and caught each other with their arms bent at impossible angles over their heads, faces contorted in irritation. They looked like complete idiots. Touche.

All three sat around the fire, not so much for warmth but as a smoke screen to ward off the relentless bugs. All three wore a hat of pine needles.

Soon, the night had settled in around them like a black hood. The roaring fire generated more than enough heat to keep the growing evening chill away, and both Jake and Claire had to shuffle back a bit to prevent the rubber on their shoes from melting.

Jake had watched the bushman lay strips of birch bark on the still hot log that had been there since they arrived. When the bark had burst into flame he stacked thick, dry branches on top of the hungry flames. Once those had been consumed, he threw on actual logs. *Now that's how to build a fire*, Jake thought.

The GEM LAKES

Claire had been recounting her near death experience in the bear caves, set off by the gigantic moose.

"Big Albert!" the bushman exclaimed, "Now there's a cranky son-of-a-gun. How's he look?"

Claire was appalled, "His name is Big Albert? He almost killed us!"

"That's what I call him. We go way back, me and Albert, almost twenty years. He almost killed me too."

"You talk to him?"

"Talk to him? He a moose! What am I, crackers? This ain't Saturday mornin' cartoons out here little lady."

Claire's face flushed red. Jake smiled, thankful he hadn't asked the same question first.

"Almost no moose ever die of old age, you know that? The wolves end up getting them eventually. I reckon they'll have a tough time with Big Albert."

The bushman looked up through the campfire smoke. "I've been keeping an eye on you two since Emerald Lake. I was impressed it took you only three hours to cross. The last poor soul that wandered though that lake sat there for ten hours straight…until the turkey vultures took him for dead and started pecking at his head. You really don't want to stand still for too long around here. Everything here is a food source for something else, including you two. The trick is to be harder to catch than the options."

Claire had never considered herself as something else's dinner, but out here, in the middle of the wild, that's exactly what she was—a ninety pound, walking, talking slab of tenderized meat. And given the "options," any animal would probably go for her before sinking its teeth into the sinewy old muscle and bone of the old man.

That made Claire think about where she was going to sleep tonight. The tent was still drying out, stretched out on a rock behind the mud hut. She was pretty sure it would start rotting if they didn't air it out properly.

"Where do you sleep?" she asked, hoping to begin a discussion about the subject.

"Right out here," the bushman said, patting the ground beside him with his hand. "Under the stars and in the fresh air."

Claire assumed he was joking. "What about the hut?"

The bushman laughed. "That place is strictly for winter. It's hot as hell's furnace in there! There's nothing to worry about out here. If it's animals you're scared of, they won't come near that fire."

Claire was unsure. There was suddenly a lot of noise coming from the forest. "Animal's sleep at night too, right?"

"Not so much."

"What do you mean?"

"Most animals are nocturnal."

"Meaning?"

"Meaning they hunt at night. But don't worry, I sleep light."

Claire stared hard at the bushman, who just leaned back on his elbows. "Besides," he continued, "There's only one animal out here that you need to really worry about."

"Which one's that?" Jake asked, his interest suddenly peaked.

"The *joaquin*. We've had a few run-ins over the years," he said thoughtfully, tapping the stump on his left arm.

"He ate your hand!" Claire yelled.

"I'm not sure how well he digested it, but yeah, he took it anyway. That's why I sleep light."

Jake motioned to Claire to close her gaping mouth. "Tell us about it," he whispered.

The old man settled back. "The *joaquin* is what the Indians called it many, many years ago. When it first appeared, it was much smaller than it is now, but even so, not something that you could really call small. The closest animal that it resembles is a cougar or a panther, only longer and thicker."

The bushman nodded to himself. "The *joaquin*, like most animals do, smells and react to fear. You might as well walk around with a dead fish in your pocket. He usually doesn't bother me much anymore, only when he's real hungry. The day this happened," pointing to his stump, "was only a month after I first came back here. The son-of-a-gun charged right at me from a hundred yards away…the speed…well he was on top of me before I could even push the safety off my gun. Before I knew it, he was trying to rip my throat out, and he would have too, but I gave him one of these," he motioned with his good hand upwards, "right in the old eyeball with my knife. An eye for a hand," he smiled grimly. "I'd say we have a mutual respect nowadays."

"But how'd you get to a hospital?" Claire asked. "You must have been miles away from anybody."

"I was. I had to build a fire…it was July but I remember shivering I was so cold, and had to stick my arm in the flames to cauterize the bleeding. I'm not going to lie to you…it was the worst pain of my life."

"What does it hunt now?"

"Anything that moves I reckon—it seems to have a hankerin' for humans. I know it hears the rants at night. The thing must be half crazy by now, trying to hunt *them* down."

"The rants?"

"You must have heard them in the bush if you made it this far. A bunch of fast talkin', rantin' and raving crazy talkers? Somewhere around the old mine?"

Jake was nodding his head. The mumblers. That's who they had heard on the shore of Sapphire Lake and who they had seen going in and out of the mine. "Who are they?"

"The rants have been here for years. Let's see now… the mine closed in '29, some months after the changes came. Anyway, the rants are the twenty-eight miners who were at the deepest point of the mine that day the magnetic field went haywire. Just like the rest of this place, they had no obvious effects…at first. Heck, they didn't even know anything had happened. But those guys got a dose of magnetic poisoning. They started losing the ability to sleep, had more energy, more strength. Two years later, when both the owner cousins were dead, they shut the place down. Those same twenty-eight guys volunteered to be the skeleton crew that stayed behind to flood the shafts and seal the opening. They didn't have much opposition. People at that time were falling like flies, mostly into the open jaws of our *joaquin* friend. Thing is, they never sealed it up. They just kept on working. Breaking rock, hauling what little ore was available without the machines. They stayed and stayed until each one dropped. But that didn't stop 'em either. They still work in that mine, day in and day out, stopping only for the Sabbath. At night, as you know, they find their way into the forest and look for something that the company may have left behind, like tools or machinery. Anything to let them keep working."

"Are you saying they're ghosts?"

"Ghosts...well I don't know about that. I just know that if they ever stopped moving, ever stopped working, ever stopped talking, that they might just evaporate into the air. I *do* know that our big cat can hear them at night and must be near mad about not being able to sink its teeth into some flesh and bone."

Claire shuddered. She missed the warm safety of her bedroom like never before. "I can't wait to get out of here."

"Oh, you can't leave," the bushman said plainly. "Not for a few nights anyway."

"What do you mean?" she asked, scared that the bushman was going to keep them as slaves. He just pointed to the sky, where the full moon loomed large in the star filled sky.

"Nobody travels these parts under a full moon...nobody with an ounce of sense anyway. You'll have to wait for the next moon cycle."

Claire's bottom lip was trembling. "We...we really have to get home...our parents must be worried."

"I'm sure they are young lady, but as I said, nobody travels these lakes under a full moon. Besides, I didn't see you drag a canoe up here. How are you getting back?"

Jake looked up in shock. He had been so focused on getting here that he hadn't thought about that particular problem. He had just assumed that Grandpa would get them back.

"Our canoe swamped, on Ruby Lake."

"Ruby! It probably hasn't even hit bottom yet!"

The GEM LAKES

"I don't understand Major. Are you telling me that you won't enter those woods at night during a full moon? Are you scared of werewolves? Are you scared of the dark? Would it help if I got you a nightlight for your hovercrafts?" Susan Lucknow spat each word as if it were its own sentence.

Major Shocklot clenched his jaw and let Mrs. Lucknow vent her frustrations.

"All I know is," she continued angrily, "that if it's light you want, then it's not going to get much lighter once this moon phase is done!"

Bob stood behind her. *A lot of things travel under a full moon Susan...not all of them with good intentions.*

"You're right ma'am. Usually, a full moon is an asset. Unfortunately, this is one of the few circumstances it is not. We're exercising caution here for everyone involved."

"Including my children?"

"Including your children ma'am." Shocklot hoped beyond hope that the frantic mother that was only inches from his face didn't take one more step forward. He felt for Susan Lucknow, but he would not tolerate being physically assaulted.

"What's out there Major? What's out there that you're so scared of? That the army is so scared of? Why don't you jump in your godforsaken planes and find my kids?"

"Mrs. Lucknow, have you heard of the Bermuda Triangle?"

She nodded while tears of frustration filled her eyes.

"Well, you've got its wicked cousin in your backyard," he said simply.

The *joaquin* was watching the bushman's camp from a safe distance, wary of its last trip through that particular opening in the forest. A powerful hunger ripped at its stomach; the smell of fresh meat had lingered on the winds through the lakes for days.

It is the largest cat in the New World, bigger by half than both the cougar and the jaguar. It has a deep-chested body, well-developed whiskers and unusually large eyes. Perhaps its most obvious feature is his very long tail, which it uses to balance itself. Like all cats, it is equipped well for killing. Its neck muscles are as strong as steel cords, and its long, sharp teeth are designed for cutting and clamping. Each forepaw has five sheathed claws, which the *joaquin* uses with deadly precision to quickly silence its prey.

In the days of the railroaders and miners, all that was needed was a bullet quick attack to break their necks with a single fatal bite.

It has been a long time since it has seen a vulnerable human in the lakes. It could sense them now, they gave off shrill vibrations of vitality, tightening its stomach and slopping drool from its long tongue. So close to the food, the *joaquin* would wait for his opportunity. It would not be long.

Jake woke up at dawn, a few hours after the bushman. He had slept terribly. Besides sleeping out in the open air for the first time ever, the blanket the old man gave him smelled of kerosene. To top it off, he couldn't get the picture of the *joaquin* out of his mind.

The old man was busy already, brewing something in the coffeepot, and chewing on a piece of dried meat.

"What's that?" Jake asked groggily.

The bushman did not even turn his head. "Are you sure you want me to answer that?"

"Yeah."

"It's moose jerky. You want some?"

"No thanks," Jake grimaced. Moose...ugh.

He shook his head. "It's better than beef. One moose is a summer's eating. You don't know what you're missing."

Jake sincerely doubted that, but sat beside the bushman anyway. "What else do you eat out here?"

The bushman stopped chewing and pondered the question for a moment. He shrugged. "Anything I can catch," he said. "Grouse, fish. Berries. If I'm lucky, maybe a deer. Stay away from fox though," he said sincerely, "Tried it once and that was once too many...there's not enough pepper in the world..."

Jake, who was not a fan of pepper anyway, grunted in acknowledgement. "Can I ask you a question?"

"I suppose..." he replied cautiously.

"What's your name?" He was getting tired of referring to him as "the bushman." It was, truth be told, a grisly sort of nickname.

"'Course I got a name...more names than you could shake a stick at. My mama wasn't one for making up her mind. Five Christian names I go by but you can't call me any of 'em."

Jake looked quizzically at him, waiting for a punchline.

"You can call me Rusty if you need to."

"Is that one of your Christian names?"

"Nope."

Again Jake waited.

"Rusty was 'bout the only name mama didn't give me. My chums used to call me that many, many years ago." He rubbed his head and pulled at his shock of pure white hair. "This used to be a terrible red."

He touched the coffeepot, which had been resting beside the hot rocks of the fire, testing to see if it had cooled enough to touch. Apparently it had because he picked it up and poured a thick, dark liquid into a battered tin cup. He looked at Jake. "You want some?"

Jake hesitated, deciding against asking for its identification. It was probably better off not knowing. Rusty poured him a cup and passed it over. It smelled.... different. He let the hot cup warm his hands and debated whether to put it to his lips.

Rusty looked at the pile of moose strips that he had cut off from a large chunk of meat and packed the remaining roast into a burlap bag. He lifted it to his shoulder and heaved it onto a tree branch that extended by the fire. As he stood up, Jake saw five good sized fish stretched out on the rock beside him. Two big pickerel and three very long northern pikes, the jaws of which were longer than Jake's face. A solid stick was poked through all five mouths, acting like a stringer.

"Where'd you get those?"

"Fishin'. Get up every mornin' before the sun. That's the best time."

"You eat those northerns?"

"Of course. This ain't a restaurant you know. I can't control what's going to bite my hook. Doesn't taste much different than pickerel anyways. Just cause it's uglier than sin don't make it any less tasty."

He lifted the wooden stringer, which must have weighed close to fifty pounds, with his good arm and hung it between two branches. Jake did not think Claire and he together could hold even one of those mighty pikes.

Their first impression of Rusty—that he was a scrawny old man, was only half the truth. He was an old man, no doubt about that, but he had lifted those fish without breaking a sweat. His body was deceivingly thin. His entire frame was muscle-packed, a combination of sharp angles and definition. With each simple movement, whether it was a light step or a heavy lift, each of the visible muscles in his body would flinch and twitch in unison. He was bone and muscle with nothing in between. That's what must come from eating a steady diet of wild game, Jake thought to himself.

"I have a question," he announced.

"Another one? No, I've never eaten children."

Jake was taken aback at first, but recovered quickly. "Actually, I was wondering about that piece of firewood you've got there. Isn't that the same piece that was there when we got here yesterday?"

Rusty was impressed. "Good eye, boy. It is the very same piece. It's rockwood."

"Rockwood?"

"There are some trees in this forest that would turn a chainsaw into spare parts in a hurry. It's easier if you just break pieces off with the flat end of an axe. That piece there has been burning for four days."

Claire had been rustled out of bed by their conversation, and made her displeasure known by standing in between them, glowering like a doberman. She saw the bushman sipping from a steaming tin cup. She wanted some of whatever it was. It probably wasn't mocha chocolate latte but she wasn't in a position to be picky.

"Could I have some?" she asked. Jake was impressed as Claire's usual morning dialogue usually consisted of one-syllable words and a series of grunts and mumbles.

He motioned to the pot.

"Great...what is it?" Oh the dreaded question.

"Blood...badger blood to be exact."

Claire lost all meaningful colour in her face. The bushman's shoulders started to heave and a smile formed on the corners of his mouth, exposing the laugh lines on his face. Jake was laughing also. He was holding a tin cup too.

"It's tree root tea...a little syrupy today but otherwise delicious. Help yourself." He chuckled again as he stood up to stretch. He took one last swig of tea and pulled out a wood handled filleting knife from the back of his belt. He started rubbing the edge against a small square of sharpening stone that he kept in his pocket.

He whistled as he worked, but Jake noticed that he stopped when he glanced up at the early morning sky. It was a lustrous pink, the sun itself a hazy orange. He was frowning.

"What's wrong?" Jake asked. *Why was he constantly watching the sky?*

"Red sky at night, sailor's delight...."

"Red sky in morning, sailor take warning," Jake finished the old verse. His father loved that saying, but hearing himself say it under a blazing salmon sky sent chills down his spine.

"We'd better get these fish to Black Pot Beach before noon. After that, well go to your Grandpa's cabin."

Jake and Claire went ahead of the bushman, down a well-worn footpath in search of berries to eat with the fish fry.

They found a patch of wild raspberrys in no time, and went to work picking enough for the three of them.

The patch, though plentiful, was small and the two Lucknows were forced to work shoulder to shoulder.

Claire found herself downwind and under Jake's arm. Her face crinkled and her eyes watered.

"Oh my God Jake....you stink!"

Jake was taken aback. "What...like what?"

"Like you haven't washed in a week!" She pinched her nose and slowly walked backwards. Jake lifted his arm and took a quick wiff. It certainly wasn't a rose garden down there.

"Check yourself out. You're not all baby powder and lilacs yourself!"

Claire turned around and gave herself the underarm test. "Oh my Gawd!"

After doing a quick leech check, they were soon swimming, clothes and all, in Black Pot Beach. The bottom was smooth flat rock with no sand or weeds. Claire was thankful for that.

The bushman rumbled down the path at the sound of water splashing. The fish swung wildly on the stringer over his shoulder. "Get out of that water! *Get out right now!*"

Jake and Claire did not ask why, as they would have if it had been their parents. The tone of the old man's voice had a desperate edge that they had not yet heard. They leaped out of the water and onto the beach.

"What! What! What's wrong?"

Black Pot Beach was actually just a lagoon, no bigger than one city block. The few trees that did surround the beach were mottled coal black like used matchsticks, leaning and bent at impossible angles. The granite rocks that formed a bowl around the water were bleached to quartz, the feldspar and mica all but washed away.

Rusty took his fish, stringer and all, and tossed it in the water. Jake and Claire looked at each other, bewildered. It wasn't like he was letting them go; they had been dead for hours!

He shaded his eyes with his hand and glanced at the position of the sun. It was hanging fat in the sky, directly over their heads; the molten orange had given way to brilliant lemon yellow. "Well, it shouldn't be too long at all."

The **GEM LAKES**

"What shouldn't be too long?" Jake regretted asking that question. Every time he had asked a question so far, he received an answer that he didn't want to hear.

"Patience, boy."

Patience was not needed. A rumble came from somewhere beneath the water, so loud that Claire checked the sky for thunderclouds. The surface of the lake started to blister, and bubbles the size of water balloons broke the surface and burst.

"Stand back."

The kids did as they were told. The water was literally boiling. Hot steam rose from the water and one of the broiled trees on the other side of the water burst into flames again.

And then...nothing. The bubbling and frothing stopped as quickly as it had started. "In the summer at least, real hot days like this, that thing can really get going. As you can see," he motioned his arm to the brown grass at their feet. "Sometimes it boils over. This is the one place I know of that doesn't ice over in winter."

Rusty waited a few more minutes for the water to cool down, and then went to retrieve his freshly cooked fish. The violent bubbling had pushed them to shore. Talk about no-hassle cooking.

"How did you do that?"

He laughed. "I didn't do nothin'. The bottom is slate and the water is shallow. When that sun gets over it and the earth works its magic, well, I guess it all comes together."

The scales of the fish peeled off easily, and Rusty made quick work of the remains. He produced the skinny filleting knife from the tattered sheath, razor sharp but pencil thin from too many turns at the sharpening stone. He chopped off the heads and tails and pulled the bones out of the soft meat. He wrapped the fillets in a pair of broad tree leaves and packed them away in a small leather pouch.

"Are you ready to visit Lake of the Clouds?"

Gordon Lucknow's grandchildren nodded their heads in nervous anticipation.

The Lake of the Clouds had a ghostlike haze that hung low near the surface of the water. It crept out into the edge of the woods like an apparition's reaching fingers. Jake could practically guarantee that *this* place was haunted.

"Pea soup," Rusty noticed. "It's better than usual."

When they were settled in the hand-carved canoe, which was twice as long as their old birch bark one, Jake could barely see the back of Claire's head. It was only an arm length away. The fog was so dense that he could physically push it away with his hands.

They could not see the dark shapes of the enormous spruce trees until they were nearly on the opposite shore. The refreshing smell of wild pine and rain filled their nostrils, even though there had been no rain since they had been drenched at the mine.

The log cabin came out of nowhere. Just like the mud hut was camouflaged in the rocks, the cabin blended in with the heavy forest that surrounded it. Compared to the Mad Trapper's shanty on Lampshine, this place looked like a four-star hotel. Each thick, yellowed spruce log had been hand cut and notched to fit snugly together. The four windows, one on each side, were not so much as cracked and the thick oak door fit tightly in its frame. This was a home.

The chimney was made of hand picked rocks and stones and the roof was covered in dull green sheets of tin. There was even a small porch off the front with a couple of small wicker chairs looking out through the trees and onto the water.

"It took us the better part of a year to put up the walls and roof," Rusty started. "The stones are mostly from around here although we did put a few moonstones in there for variety. Made 'er look nice, eh? The tin came from the old miner's cabins. It took us a week to hammer the dents out of 'em. Go on, take a look inside."

Jake stood in front of the door with his heart in his stomach and a lump in his throat. He was not sure why. When he touched the smooth wooden door handle he waited just a moment before pushing it open. He was about to open an unknown chapter of his family's history.

Claire was practically hanging on his back, pushing him through the threshold. "I want to see too! Move it!" Patience was not a virtue that had been bestowed upon his sister. "Oh my gosh..."

The cabin was basically one big room and its warmth immediately struck Jake. Even though the charred coals in the stone fireplace looked cold, the air in the cabin was still more than comfortable and seemed to keep the chill of the outside air at bay. Perhaps those ashes had been Grandpa's last fire.

There was a bed in the far corner, on the left side of the fireplace. A small wooden table was bare except for a fire-scarred coffeepot and two metal cups that had been cleaned and stacked neatly, waiting for the next mornings use. Jake's eyes stung. That morning had never come for Grandpa.

"Spent many a fine hour sitting at that very table. Playing cards through the night, in front of a nice fire and a hot cup of coffee." Rusty seemed to be lost in his thoughts, his eyes were open but glazed over, like he was looking back thought the past. "At Christmas, we used to splash a little rum in there...yeah, I do miss those days already."

An old coat hung on a peg on the back of the door. It was faded tan with big brown buttons down the front. One of the buttons was missing and had never been replaced. Grandpa's jacket?

Shelves had been carved into the log walls—some held a few brilliant moonstones that were so shiny that Jake could see his reflection in them. There were a few whittled pieces of driftwood in the shapes of animals and a small pile of books on the shelf below that.

Mounted on the wall was a delicate wood carving of an owl that was so detailed and precise that Jake wondered how a human being could create such a thing.

"Did Grandpa make this?"

Rusty shook his head. "No. He did those pieces on the shelf. He was just taking it up. An old friend on Lampshine gave the owl to him. Your grandfather was friends with the entire lake. Everybody knew him. He kept the owl to remind him of those friends. Beautiful isn't it?"

It truly was. The entire cabin was beautiful in its own right. Jake felt a whole lot better knowing that Grandpa hadn't lived in a barren mud hut all those years. It would make his dad really happy to hear about this.

"Why don't you have a place like this?" Claire asked Rusty.

The old man grunted. "I'm happy where I am. Got no need for a fancy place."

Jake looked around the cabin again, trying to soak up every little detail so he could tell his dad.

When it was time to leave, Jake made sure the door was shut tight. They stood on the porch that looked out into the Lake of the Clouds. Jake's mind raced. All this time, Grandpa had been alive! Incredible!

When they returned to camp, Rusty took out an ancient barbecue grill and laid the fish fillets neatly over the fire. "We've got to crisp this up some," he said, possibly to himself. Claire went back to her makeshift bed and napped in the afternoon sun. Jake stayed and helped Rusty with the fish.

"So you've got it in you too, do you boy?"

Jake was stunned. What? Did he have TUMOUR stamped on his forehead or something?

"You know, the human body is the greatest machine on earth. It can last decades with just one pump and can heal itself, to a degree, in a matter of days. Unfortunately, as in your case, and your granddad's, it can sometimes be a mite too aggressive, growin' cells that it can't control. Not so diff'rent than having a Dr. Frankenstein in there somewhere."

The next sentence out of Rusty's mouth would change Jake's life forever. "Your cancer can't survive out here. You *do* know that don't you?"

The GEM LAKES

Jake looked at him blankly. He had *felt* it. He had *sensed* it—he just hadn't allowed himself to believe it. He had walked and paddled all this way with minimum sleep and a serious lack of food and felt better than he had in a year.

"You have felt the change, haven't you?" Rusty continued. "It's a basic property of magnetic fields. You're standing on one, by the way. It's forcing the electrical charges in your brain into a spiraling motion, back and forth, back and forth, trapping them where they are. Your tumour can never grow bigger. Not out here."

"How do you know that?"

"Look at your grandfather. Besides that, I haven't been out here forever you know. I did go to university back in the day. I don't think simple physics has changed much in the last few decades."

Jake was tired of talking about the whole 'how' of it all. "Well why does it have to be in me in the first place?"

"It's not just in you, not by far. And the hundreds of thousands of others don't have a refuge like this. They don't have that option. You can look at it one of two ways; that you're one of the unluckiest people on the face of the earth...or you're the luckiest."

"I guess so..."

"I know so."

"I guess I just don't understand why it happened to me."

"Why? Why not? What makes you so special?"

"It's just not...fair!" He sputtered.

"Fair? Son, what level are you at in school?"

"Grade seven."

"Uh hum. And after that you'll go to high school, date all the cheerleaders, go to college, injure your knee, take years and years of corporate law and spend the rest of your life in a cramped office trying to get yourself out of debt and ready for retirement at age ninety-two when you'll have to replace all your organs and joints with plastic parts. Sounds great!"

Nobody had ever confronted him about his sickness. Everybody had just considered it as a death sentence. A sudden end to a promising life…a tragedy. Maybe it didn't have to be that way.

"What about you?" Jake countered, "Don't you have a family? Why didn't you just stay with them till the end huh? You probably just ran away."

The old man silently pulled a long spear-like branch from the pile beside him. Jake was sure that he was going to run him through with it.

He didn't. He just snapped it in half, stirring the embers with one and throwing the other on the fire.

"Son, I said goodbye to my family…I just wasn't ready to say goodbye to myself."

Jake, now faced with an option to live, was suddenly very leery of dying. When there had been no option, no chance, no hope, Jake had not dared to create one in his head. He hadn't wanted to waste one more second on thinking about the future when there was no possibility of one and his seconds had become just as precious as years.

The only question now was that if he wanted to live, it would be under a much different setting than he would have planned. Still, considering the alternative, it didn't seem like much of a question at all.

Rusty spoke again, more softly this time, "On the old path of life, a whole lot of folks get bumped right off on their way to where they think they're going. You just got pushed down another path, that's all. That path might lead right up to a certain cabin on Lake of the Clouds."

"What about Claire? She can't stay here."

"I'll take her back myself," he said, "No grandchild of Gord Lucknow will come into harm's way on my watch. I can assure you that."

Jake was not acting like himself. Claire could tell that much right away. He had not asked a question or even said a word in hours and that in itself was enough to ring the warning bells.

But his skin was pale too, and he was pacing. Jake never paced.

They would be leaving here tomorrow and if Jake was feeling sick again, well...she didn't think she could take one more night out here. She pulled him aside.

"Are you feeling all right?"

"What do you mean?"

"You know...your...are you feeling okay to make it back?"

Jake's eyes seemed lost in space. Claire wondered if he had been taking his pills. Come to think of it, she hadn't seen that red bottle of pills in quite a few days.

"Where are your pills?"

He just shrugged. "I don't think I'm going to go with you." Claire thought she must have misheard him. "Say again?"

Jake cleared his throat. "I think I'm going to stay here."

"You can't stay here...outside like this! We have to go home!"

He replied, "Why?"

Claire resisted the almost overpowering urge to smack some sense into her younger brother. Sometimes, sisters had to do that, to shake the cobwebs loose. "Because you can't live in the bush! Not to mention Mom would kill you!" She regretted that phrase the moment it left her mouth.

"She might not get the chance if I go back."

"What?"

"Haven't you noticed that I haven't been tired out here? That I can go to bed late and get up early and not need a five hour nap in between? Haven't you noticed that I haven't had a pill in days and I haven't blacked out either?"

"You passed out on Ruby Lake!"

"Only because you flipped the canoe and I had to save your life! Superman would have passed out after that swim!" He took pause for a moment and corrected himself. "All right—maybe not Superman, but for sure Batman."

"So you want me to go back all by myself?" Jake had worked the guilt card to get her out here. She would use it to get him back.

"Rusty said he'll take you home, in his canoe."

"Oh that's great! What do you want me to tell Mom and Dad? As if they won't come looking for you?"

"They aren't looking for us now are they?"

"How do you know?" she shot back angrily.

"C'mon Claire, it's not like we've wandered off the trails. They're overgrown but they're still there. How hard would it be?"

Claire decided that it was easier to cry than think about that. Her eyes flooded.

Jake grabbed her shoulders. "Look how long Grandpa lived out here! He only died a few days ago. He had cancer too. Maybe Rusty is right. Maybe I can have a life here. What have I got to lose? Die here or die there, what's the freakin' difference?"

Claire had enough of this conversation. She turned around and stormed off in the opposite direction.

Dinner that night was noticeably quieter. The two siblings sat on opposite sides of the fire and did not make eye contact. On the menu—the biggest jackrabbit that either child had ever seen, even in the movies. Jake's first pet when he was young was a rabbit named Thumper. He took one long look at the rabbit meat, its bloody juices dripping down the forked stick, and then decided that he might vomit.

He waved his hand when the old man offered him a portion and trodded off towards the forest, in search of something more appealing. The trapper shrugged and gave Claire a look like "more for us." Claire gingerly took her half of the rabbit and promptly stuck it back on the stick and charred it on the flames. She was desperately hungry and could never have imagined eating a rabbit only a week ago. Now, the smell of meat made her mouth water and her stomach cramp in anticipation. She was far less picky about her food than her brother. He was very resourceful and she had no doubt that he would find something to his liking.

Sure enough, just as Claire had retrieved her black encrusted meat from the fire, Jake returned with his baseball cap half full of acorns.

The GEM LAKES

He said nothing as he dumped the nuts from his hat to the iron pan and, purely to give the impression that he knew what he was doing, sprinkled fresh green pine needles over them, to add flavour.

He pan-roasted them over the fire and proudly displayed them in his tin plate when they were done, slightly blackened and piping hot.

He popped one into his mouth after a sufficient cooling time had passed and crunched down on the wild nut. Peanuts or almonds it was not. The bitterness drilled him right between the eyes and he spat the vile squirrel staple across the fire and into the lap of his sister.

"Eeeww."

The bushman stifled a snorting laugh.

"Boil 'em."

Jake's tongue felt like he had licked paper mache.

"What?"

"Boil 'em...more than once. You can roast 'em, broast 'em, toast 'em or set them out it the sun from now till next Tuesday, but you won't rid 'em of the bitterness unless you boil 'em....more than once."

Claire looked up. The new moon had arrived. She found the total blackness intolerable and crept as close to the fire as possible, even though it meant sitting closer to Jake who she was still not talking to. After finally drying out properly, the tent had been set up on the rock beside the mud hut. Claire would not be sleeping under a moon-less sky—that was for sure.

At the same time, she couldn't take her eyes off the star-filled sky. She only knew one constellation, the Big Dipper, and picked it out easily. Rusty picked out half a dozen before Jake finally called him on one.

"That is not Orion's Belt," he challenged.

Rusty pursed his lips. "Say's you. I say it is. I also say that I can find my own constellations. Who's out here to tell me otherwise?"

Jake thought about that. It was true.

"Take those five right up there," he pointed to a group of especially bright stars that seemed to take light from each other.

"I named that one Lucknow...for your Grandpa, because he lived such a bright and full life when he came back here."

Jake stared at the Lucknow cluster for a moment but was distracted by something else...something much bigger than stars.

Long curtains of pulsating light had formed in the northern sky. White, green and purple beams danced and radiated on a blanket of blackness. Claire saw it too. "Oh my God..."

Rusty looked over his shoulder and smiled.

"The Northern Lights. Have you ever seen such a thing?"

Neither Jake nor Claire could answer. They were awestruck. They had seen the Northern Lights, of course, but they had never seen them like this. Jake had a sense of being enveloped with warmth from the lights, like the pulsating was actually breathing. They lasted for an hour, in which time not a word was spoken. No words were needed for they were listening to a silent symphony that each was trying to burn in their minds forever.

Claire woke up. What was wrong? Then she realized that the nightsounds had stopped, even the frogs. She opened the flap of the tent to see Rusty crouching by the fire, a huge hunting knife in one hand and a long, bony finger over his lips, urging for silence, like he was straining to hear something. She could make out the outline of Jake sitting up behind him, as still as a stone statue.

Then she heard it too—a movement of air, a soft crunch on the ground, then another. Something brushed slightly against the side of the tent. Rusty's head never moved but his eyes followed the sound. Finally, Claire could take no more, "What is it?" she whispered.

"The *joaquin*," the bushman said with such certainty that it startled her. Without moving his head, he silently pulled two smaller knives out of his pack; one was the filleting knife, the other, an ancient looking Swiss Army piece that was missing almost all the attachments. The big blade was still there, however, and he flipped it out. He tossed the filleting knife to Jake and the other to Claire. Claire knew she was not going to like what he was going to say next.

The GEM LAKES

"Promise me one thing. Whatever comes through your tent, you fight until the end…don't run; you won't get far. Fight until the noise is over."

Jake clenched his weapon ready for the fight of his life. At least he had a chance to fight this threat.

Claire remembered that Rusty had said that animals smelled fear. If that were the case, she must be giving of the vibes of a bag full of garlic. She gripped the small knife with both hands, quite unsure how to go about defending herself from a man-eating cat.

Claire realized now that the worst part of dying was the anticipation of dying. Whatever happened, she wished it would just be over. That was when the *joaquin* tore through the back entrance of the paper-thin tent.

The tent sliced neatly in two and something knocked Claire back into one of the halves, wrapping her up in the canvas as she hurtled backwards. The more she struggled to free herself, the tighter she became trapped. She stopped moving and just listened.

The great cat hissed and growled from deep in its powerful throat. Before Jake or Rusty could move, the *joaquin* charged and hit Rusty square in the chest and rolled on top of him, man and cat a blurred somersault of flesh and fur.

The wildcat had Rusty's already shortened arm in his jaws and was shaking it side to side, like he was trying to tear it off. Rusty looked like a rag doll being thrown to either side but he managed to get his good hand free and pummeled the handle of his knife into the cat's soft nose. It let out a bloodcurdling screech and swatted him on the side of the face with a giant paw. Jake thought he heard bones crack.

Jake could not see where Claire was, although he assumed she was the lumpy mass hiding underneath the tent. The *joaquin* had turned away from Rusty's limp body and squared himself towards Jake. A river of drool ran between its elongated fangs. Jake clutched the old filleting knife and put it out in front of him, like he was drawing a sword. It looked terribly feeble against the hideous size of the *joaquin*. The cat took three deliberate steps towards him. Its padded feet did not make even the slightest sound which Jake, oddly, found the most unnerving feature about the animal.

He could hear the swish of the *joaquin's* tail cut through the night air, and the terrible primal whine that generated somewhere deep in its aching belly.

Jake had never been more scared than this in his life, even when the doctors had told him point-blank that he was going to die. He was somewhat relieved, however, that he was not the deer-caught-in-headlights kind of scared and he was able to think clearly. Clearer than usual in fact. He held the flimsy filleting knife up with as much authority as he could muster and then barked loudly at the approaching predator.

The *joaquin* barely lifted his head, his one eye widened slightly in what may have been mild amusement. The boy was resisting. There were only two living things that had ever escaped the *joaquin*. One was the old man. The second was actually the first, a wolverine by the shore of Ruby Lake. The *joaquin* had cornered it between the water and a rock shelf and the animal had hissed and spat at him with such a fury that the big cat had begun to consider backing off. Then the wolverine attacked *him*. It had been the size of a small bear with the strength to match. Pound-for-pound it was the strongest and fiercest animal the hunter had ever come across. He had not gone after wolverine ever since, and that had been over thirty years ago.

The barking from the boy reminded the cat only vaguely of that encounter. He did not expect much of a fight from this frail-looking prey.

The *joaquin* hunted like all wildcats do, stalking their prey to within easy lunging distance and then pouncing, claws unsheathed and jaws wide open, going for the vital blood vessels in the neck to dispatch their prey easily. Jake subconsciously lowered his chin into his chest and stood his ground. He had a plan.

The cat progressed towards him steadily, and Jake waited until he sped up before bracing himself for his final move. The killer cat launched himself through the night air easily, and Jake dropped to the ground while thrusting his knife hand upwards with all his strength. The momentum of the cat took it over Jake's body and it landed on all fours behind him. Jake rolled once and then looked back to see the feline hunter staring straight at him.

The knife was no longer in Jake's hand. Jake sat there, defenceless. The cat lurched towards him, but its front legs buckled and he crashed to the ground. His one eye blinked, then rolled into the back of his head.

At the first light of dawn, Rusty opened his eyes and propped himself up on his elbows, wincing at the pain of his arm.

"Stupid cat..." he muttered, "It already had that hand." He looked at Jake and Claire with a slight look of surprise. That graduated into full blown shock when he looked past them and saw the long thick tail of the *joaquin* poking out of the grass.

"What happened? Are you all right?"

"Better than you. Your head's bleeding."

Rusty just waved them off, and pushed himself up off the ground if not a little unsteadily. He brushed past them and shuffled his way towards the body.

Rusty wondered if the old cat had just dropped dead of a heart attack, too old to be chasing people around anymore. He lifted the tail of the old beast, and heard Jake make an audible sigh.

Then he kicked it on its side, and noticed the filleting knife handle jutting out of its chest, the blade sunk right between its ribs, right near its lungs. It had been a shot in a million for that blade not to have snapped like a toothpick.

"You know, Lake of the Clouds is not the fountain of youth...as you can see," he started, and then waved an arm in front of himself. "But I'll tell you what...I'm one hundred and five years old and if I do say so myself, I don't feel a day over eighty."

Jake stopped what he was doing (trying to break a chunk of rockwood into a manageable piece) and listened.

"Everything dies, it's a part of nature that you can't do anything about. Well I'm still waiting but I ain't going to go look for it."

A light went on in Claire's head. What they had stumbled on out here was an opportunity, plain and simple. For Jake to turn away from it would not only be foolish but a death sentence. She wanted him to come back for her not for him. That suddenly seemed very selfish.

She looked at him. "Will you send me a message in a bottle or something?"

Jake, for the first time that he could remember, started crying in front of his sister. Not just a little sniffle either, but a shoulder heavin', eyes-floodin', water-works special and he didn't feel the least bit embarrassed about it either. This, of course, set Claire off on a similar spectacle and the two hugged so tightly that their wet cheeks mashed together.

Rusty, who was nearly provoked to tears himself by the whole demonstration, turned and walked towards the bush to give them some privacy.

He reappeared an hour later carrying a canoe over his head, obviously no worse the wear from his encounter last night.

"It's time," he said.

So this was it. Claire was on the verge of gushing into an emotional diatribe which she knew from past experience might collapse into a series of over-the-top think-of-me-when-the-wind-blows type of comments that were better off left in bad movies.

She had nothing to pack. With the tent now shredded they had officially lost everything that they had come out with except the clothes on their backs.

They did not embrace this time, both fearful that they wouldn't be able to let each other go.

"I hate long goodbyes," Rusty prodded. He felt sorry for them but lingering around sure wasn't going to help anything.

"Goodbye Jake."

"Bye Claire."

The GEM LAKES

The scene at the northeast corner of Timber Wolf Lake could not have looked more contradictory. On the dead calm of the morning water, a light mist of fog was steaming up off the night-cooled lake. And then there was the convoy of army boats, contrasting against the serenity of nature like black strokes of tar over a Van Gogh. The hulking bulk of the boats, the black and coldness of the steel armour and the sheer number of camouflaged soldiers who were completely surrounding the portage into Opal, looked like they were in a nose-to-nose standoff against the bullrushes. The folks who declared this area a wilderness zone seventy years back would be rolling in their graves.

Bob Lucknow, standing on the hull of the lead boat, wouldn't have been surprised if they had a couple of submarines under the surface of the lake as well.

Each soldier was decked out in full fatigues, complete with a smear of black and green paint on his face. They looked even more menacing than any animal that Bob could remember seeing back there. Even more ominous was the weaponry of the army Rangers. What exactly were they expecting back there?

Standing beside Bob, Major Shocklot's face looked grim. In the military, you did not move against your enemy if you didn't know who your enemy was. They were used to having intelligence information to plan their attacks carefully. This was a rescue mission against an unknown entity, and that was the most dangerous kind of all.

Duncan Shocklot could only think about the missing miners, the murdered railroad men and the maimed hydro crews. They were a group of men who *knew* the bush and could take care of themselves and yet were easily dispatched by a never seen predator. The downed bush pilots weighed heavily on his mind. There were others as well, incidents long since sealed in the bowels of the defense departments' most remote warehouses. He would not take a chance with his pilots. He had called off air support an hour ago. Technology be damned, these lakes were a menace to his men. He would lead them on the ground. Of course, he had no way of knowing that a fifteen-year old boy had already killed the legendary beast with a mere fishing knife.

Then, as the Major raised his arm above his head and was about to motion the unit forward, he stopped in mid air. Sixty-two men simultaneously raised their automatic weapons and leveled them at some movement in the trees. Little Claire Lucknow, looking exhausted and sunburned but otherwise okay, took one look at the commotion in front of her and fainted.

Bob Lucknow started a fire for the first time this season, more for the comfort than for the warmth. Claire, huddled in the blanket from Jake's top bunk, looked like she could use a little of both. Major Shocklot had demanded an immediate debriefing from Claire, and after three hours of that, she had went straight to bed.

She had just awoken from a six-hour 'nap', her eyes still sleepy and tired. She held a steaming cup of hot chocolate with both hands, the marshmallows melting into a gooey gob on the top.

Bob had put Susan to bed only an hour ago with the aid of some sleeping tranquilizers that the military medic had given him. Despite the joy of Claire returning and the anguish of Jake still missing, Susan had passed out as soon as her head had hit the pillow. He would have a long few days ahead of him as he tried to explain to her where Jake was and how he could never come back.

It was ironic really, because both Bob and Susan had braced themselves for so long for the day that Jake would be gone that this was going to take some getting used to. He was still gone and yet he wasn't. They had to be thankful that he was still alive and yet...live their lives without him. Yes, it would be a tough road ahead but somehow, it just seemed to get a little less bumpy.

"Dad?"

"Yeah hon?"

"Do you think Jake...well...do you think he'll be okay?"

Bob pulled a photograph out of his jacket pocket, the one he had carried with him in that exact spot for over twenty-five years. It was dulled in colour, a little smooth around the edges but otherwise in perfect condition. He passed it to Claire.

The picture was of three men, one of them a younger version of her father. "Yes, that's me in the middle. Look at that hair..." he said wistfully.

The Mad Trapper, younger to be sure but still a bag of bones as far as Claire could tell, was on her father's left. She wondered if he had been born with that many crevasses in his face. Rusty was on his right, with both hands at that time. "That's your grandfather," he said, pointing to the man they at first called the bushman, carefully watching Claire's face for a reaction. Claire had heard the words but did not comprehend them for a while. The sentence took more than a minute to wrap around her brain.

Finally she asked, "When was this taken?"

"About twenty-five years ago, when they first went back. About six months after Dad was diagnosed."

Claire jabbed a finger at the picture. "But he said that Grandpa had died. He showed us his grave."

"The grave is of the man who took this picture...Chipper Prefontaine. He rescued Grandpa from the bear caves once."

"But why would he lie? Why wouldn't he tell us? Didn't he like us?"

"Whoa, whoa hon, slow down. He's legally dead you know. He left this life behind a very long time ago. It's hard on him as well you know, to let himself step back into it. And you were going to spill that little secret to the Major. He probably would have wormed it out of you during that debriefing." Claire smiled out the side of her mouth. It did not take much for her to crumble under confrontation. "That's a lot of emotion for a little girl to carry." Bob spoke from his own experience, and the sometimes overwhelming pressures of knowing that his father had been alive while everybody else thought him dead.

"He lived in that mud hut all this time? That's sad."

Bob shook his head. "That was Chipper's hut. He was the type of guy who lived off the land. That was his life. I'm sorry to hear that he passed away. Your grandpa lives in a cabin on Lake of the Clouds—if you found him at the hut, he was probably getting Chipper's things in order. They were good friends."

Claire was beginning to understand.

Gordon Francis Emmanuel Clarence Xavier Lucknow had been gone for over twenty-five years and yet there had never been a funeral for him. By law (after ten years, a missing person is declared legally dead) they could have, but Bob was the only one that had known that the reason they didn't have a body to bury was that the body was still breathing.

"You knew...why didn't you ever tell us?"

Bob looked her in the eyes, "I suppose to prevent what happened from happening...it is not a safe place to visit. It's especially no place for kids."

Bob had stopped going back into the Gem Lakes with the Mad Trapper to visit his father the year Claire was born and the journey became too risky for a new father with new responsibilities. Every few months, Bob would meet his father at the bullrushes and bring him a few supplies, not much, maybe some lantern oil one time, some fresh socks another, stuff like that.

And every once in a while, fishing on Timber Wolf before the sun would set, there his dad would be, waving and watching from the Opal Portage...just checking in.

Basically, Rusty Lucknow, by starting new life, had to let go of the old one.

"Do you think he'll tell Jake?"

He smiled, "I'm sure it will be a very long night at the campfire tonight."

Claire was silent, watching their own fire flicker and crack. "Are you going to tell Mom? It would probably help her a lot to know that he was being taken care of."

"Of course I'll tell her."

The crow, so large that cottagers often mistook it for a raven, squawked loudly into the fresh lake air. The sound carried for miles. It had watched the journey of the Lucknow children with interest. The old bird had seen many things over the years, from the first railway spike being hammered in, to the Morley tragedy years later and many, many things in between.

It had even seen the magic of the Gem Lakes, where humans like Rusty, Chipper Prefontaine and a handful of others before them, led long and satisfying lives—years after their respective afflictions would have overcome them.

If Jake's sickness behaved—the same as his grandfather's, the boy might live to be a hundred, maybe older. He could easily outlive both his parents and his sister, and every friend he had ever had in school, including Melissa Murray.

This particular crow was getting old. It expected it had enough time to see how Jake would fare with life in the forest. Time, however, passed slowly in the woods and, not discounting how far back the crow could see in the past, it had no vision into the future.

For Jake, and the rest of the Lucknows, the rest of summer started now.